About the Author

I was raised in Italy until the age of nine and then in upstate NY. I studied and taught at a university in Syracuse. I've written several works of fiction and poetry, and have also painted.

A Sense of Humor

paul devito

A Sense of Humor

Olympia Publishers
London

www.olympiapublishers.com
OLYMPIA PAPERBACK EDITION

A CIP catalogue record for this title is
available from the British Library.

ISBN: 978-1-80074-508-7

This is a work of fiction.
Names, characters, places and incidents originate from the writer's
imagination. Any resemblance to actual persons, living or dead, is
purely coincidental.

First Published in 2022

Olympia Publishers
Tallis House
2 Tallis Street
London
EC4Y 0AB

Printed in Great Britain

Dedication

I dedicate this book to, James Owens.

A Sense of Humor

She was tall, dark-haired, slender, and beautiful. Her name was Patricia, and we were in graduate school together. She was in the Communication School, and I was in English. We had gone out for about eight months, when she called to break it off. I was jealous.

"I wasn't flirting with him!" she said.

"What do you call it?" I asked.

"We were talking. Aren't I allowed to talk to other men?"

"Of course, but he's different. You went out with him last year."

"I don't want to have sex with him any more," she said. "We broke up for a reason."

We were sitting in her living room. It was evening, and the light from the lamp was dim.

"I need some space," I said.

"You're breaking up with me?" she asked.

"No, only for a while. I need to think about this. It's not the first time it's happened."

"Fine. See what I care. I'm tired of this relationship anyway," she said.

"You sound like a child," I said.

"So do you."

I left abruptly and drove home, somewhat relieved. I lived in a very small apartment with enough room for a bed, chair, and television. I was close enough to campus to walk, but Patricia's apartment was relatively far away. I felt frustrated and angry, and thought that I would probably miss her. As soon as I got home, I called her.

"Hi," she said. "What's up?"

"I'm sorry," I said. "I didn't mean to be so rude. Of course you can talk to other men, but you must understand how I feel."

"I understand, and I'm sorry, too. I won't talk to Mark any more."

"Good! Now, maybe we can stay together," I said.

"Sure. Why don't you come back and spend the night?"

"Fine," I said.

I went back to her place, and we watched a movie on television, avoiding our homework. We were still excited about each other sexually, so we made love after the movie. It was the best sex I had ever had. We fell asleep and slept soundly through the night. I had classes early in the morning and didn't wake her when I got up. I showered at her place, and I drove to school. My first class was Modern English Literature with a professor named Laura. Laura was blonde and quite attractive. She wore nice clothes and led our discussion gracefully. I was twenty-six, and she was thirty-two. We were talking about Virginia Woolf, and the discussion was getting interesting.

"She was a feminist," Sarah said. "Her female characters were strong and very complex."

"I don't think she was that much of a feminist," Brad said. "She didn't write much about women's rights."

The discussion went that way for a while, and I kept staring at Laura. After class, I went up to her and said that I needed to talk to her sometime about the material. She told me her office hours, and we made an appointment to meet. I was excited, and I wondered if she could notice my nervousness. I went to my next two classes; then I went home. As soon as I got home, I called

Pat.

"Hi, honey," she said.

"Hi, yourself," I said. "Did you miss me?"

"Not really," she said, laughing.

"Do you want to have lunch?" I asked.

"I can't. I have to work on a presentation, but we can have dinner together, and if you want, you can spend the night again."

"Okay, I'll call you later."

I was thinking about having sex with Pat that night, but I was also thinking about Laura. Pat was smart and quick, but Laura was a real intellectual, which attracted me. I was reading *To the Lighthouse*, and that afternoon, I spent the whole time reading. It was my favorite novel, and Virginia was my favorite author. I fell asleep reading and woke up at about six. I called Pat and told her I was coming over. When I arrived, she was in her negligee.

"Do you have something in mind?" I asked.

"I want to study your anatomy," she said.

We made love in the shower, and it was great. Sometimes I thought I wanted to marry her, but knew it was only because the sex was so good. She would have made a good wife, but I didn't feel I was in love with her. I thought I was in love with Laura. Laura fascinated me because she knew so much more than I did. There was something competitive in my nature that loved the challenge of conquering a superior mind. I was a good actor though, and Pat never suspected.

"What do you want for dinner?" Pat said.

"A salad is fine for me. Don't go to any trouble."

She made a salad while I sat at the kitchen table. Her apartment was much better than mine because her father was a doctor and could afford it. She had beautiful curtains on the windows and comfortable contemporary furniture, all in blue.

She had plants, and everything was neat.

"Did you do anything interesting in class today?" she said.

"Yeah. We talked about how language is caught between metaphor and literality."

"That's beyond me," she said.

"I know you're not interested in literary theory, but I'll explain it to you sometime," I said.

"I'm interested in theory, but you can't throw a difficult concept at me and expect me to understand it."

I was thinking that Laura wouldn't have any trouble understanding it, but I didn't say anything.

"I got my presentation finished," Pat said.

"That's great," I said. "You also made a good presentation in the shower."

"Sex is the only reason you like me," she said.

"You know that's not true."

"Why else do you like me?"

"You're very smart and strong," I said, "and you take good care of me."

"You don't deserve it."

"Stop now," I said.

"Okay, but I'm watching you, mister."

We ate our salad, and she had put all kinds of wonderful things in it. I wondered if Laura would take as good care of me. I hated thinking about Laura when I was with Pat, but I couldn't help it.

"I want to live in New York City," Pat stated.

"We can do that," I said. "I've got two more years for my Master's, and then I could apply to schools in the city."

"Syracuse is a good place for school, but not a good place to live," she said.

"My family is here. That's why I'm here. I got lucky to find a good program," I said.

"Your mom is great. So is your brother."

"We should take a trip to Westchester so I can meet your family," I said.

"We will. You can play basketball with my brothers."

"I want to meet your parents," I said.

"They'll like you."

"Do you want to study or watch a movie?" I asked.

"Watch a movie. I finished my work for the day."

"I'm going to read," I said, "but the TV won't bother me."

We hung out together for a few hours, then went to bed. We had great sex again, and I forgot all about Laura for the night.

Chapter II

I had a dream early in the morning, but I could only remember bits and pieces of it. I remember that I was in bed with both Laura and Pat. I was making love to both of them, when Pat got up and started screaming at me. Then Laura lectured me about infidelity. That's all I could remember. The dream was disturbing, but I laughed to myself about it. I didn't tell Pat, of course, but I knew that if Laura was in my dreams, then I was in love with her. Pat got up when I got up, and we showered together. We made love again, and it was intense. I really enjoyed morning sex. After we got dressed, I made some coffee, and we sat at her kitchen table talking.

"I like it when you fuck me in the shower," she said. "The water is so sensuous."

"You come more easily in the shower," I said.

"You're a good lover," she said.

"I learned from you."

"What's going on today?" she asked.

"I have two classes, and I have to finish this novel."

"You have theory today, don't you?" she said.

"Yes, but I'm behind on my reading. I have read every page five times just to get the gist of it."

"I don't even understand why you like that stuff," she said.

"It's fascinating, but you have to ease into it and be taught by a good professor."

"I never liked philosophy," she said.

"Well, you're going to be a star on television. You don't have to worry too much about philosophy, except maybe ethics."

"That sounded condescending."

"Pat, I didn't mean it that way. I meant that metaphysics isn't going to affect your life."

"Don't worry — my pretty little head is what I heard," she said.

"Come on now. I told you ethics is what you have to concentrate on."

"We discuss ethics in our program," she said.

"I'm sure you do. It's probably the most important branch of philosophy."

"But you're interested in metaphysics," she said.

"And ontology. They all relate to language now. That's how literary theory comes in."

"Well, let's talk about something else. I don't want to worry my pretty little head about philosophy."

"I have to go," I said.

"Bye," she said.

I had a meeting with Laura, and I wasn't going to be late. She was six years older than I, which intrigued me and made it more of a challenge. She was sitting in her small office with a single lamp on her desk.

"Hi," she said.

"I wanted to discuss Virginia Woolf with you," I said. "I don't know much about her life, but I know she had a tragic death."

"What would you like to know?" she said.

"Was she happily married?" I asked.

"For the most part, I guess, but she had her problems, like all of us."

"Are you married?" I asked.

15

I wanted desperately to get off the subject of Virginia Woolf and talk about something personal.

"I'm engaged." She smiled.

I saw the big ring on her finger and figured he had some money and prestige.

"Congratulations," I said. "How long has it been?"

"Four years."

"That's a long time."

"He teaches at Yale. It's hard for us," she said.

"Long distance relationships are hard," I agreed.

"I wanted to ask you something," I said. "I wrote a novel last year. Would you be willing to read it?"

"Sure. I'd love to. I write poetry. Maybe you'd like to read some," she said.

"I'd be thrilled. I can't stay, but I'd like to set up another meeting so we can exchange our writing."

"How about the same time next week?" she said.

"That would be great. I'll see you later."

I walked out of her office feeling elated. She had qualities that I had never seen in another woman. Her facial expressions were so subtle, and her smile was so gentle. I could tell she liked me, but I couldn't tell how much. I couldn't wait to show her my novel. I knew she would give me an informed opinion. I went to my theory class and paid close attention. It was fascinating to hear the different theories of fiction. De Man said that fiction already knows language is false. I thought about this for a while and decided that language can also be true to some extent. It was a mixture of the two in some weird fashion. I went back to Pat's apartment, but she was already gone. I made a salad for lunch and listened to music while I ate. My meeting with Laura echoed in my mind, and I knew I liked her better than I liked Pat. This was a predicament. Patricia returned a few hours later, and she kissed me when she came in the door.

"How were your classes?" she said.

"I skipped Eighteenth Century Literature," I said.

"Why?"

"I haven't read Pope's *The Rape of the Lock*, and I didn't want to go to class unprepared."

"How was theory?" she asked.

"Great, as usual."

"I'm so excited about this television program we're shooting," she said.

"I'm glad."

She ate a sandwich, and we sat in the living room watching the news. She was so sexy sitting there that I put my head on her lap.

"Will you marry me?" she said.

My heart started pounding.

"Yes," I responded.

"Then we're engaged," she said happily.

"You realize we've only been going out for eight months," I said.

"It was love at first sight for me," she said.

"Me, too. Do you want to make love?"

"Naturally," she said.

We made love, and I was upset with myself for thinking about Laura. I knew Laura was engaged, but I still felt I had a chance with her. I made Pat orgasm and came inside her for the first time.

"Hey, what are you doing?" she said.

"We're engaged now," I said.

"I don't want to have a child yet."

"I wasn't really planning to. It just happened."

"You have to be more careful," she said.

"I will. I promise."

"I'm going on the pill."

"Good idea," I said. "I hate pulling out."

"I can tell." She laughed. "I'm going to the bathroom to wash myself."

I lay on the bed exhausted and perfectly satisfied, though I hoped she wasn't pregnant. I thought immediately about Laura and wondered what she was like in bed. Pat was in the bathroom for quite a while, so I put my clothes on even though I was going to shower. Finally, she came out.

"I hope I'm not pregnant. I don't know what I'll do if I am."

"What time of the month are you?" I asked.

"Right in the middle."

"That's not good."

"I know. That's why I'm worried. I'm going to the clinic tomorrow."

"Have you been on the pills before?" I asked.

"Yeah, a couple of times," she said. "They're really not good for you."

I took a shower and thought about Laura the whole time. I knew I shouldn't have agreed to marry Patricia, but I was caught up in the moment. I would see how I felt in the future. Pat and I stayed up for an hour or two more, then we went to bed. Later in the night, she woke me up.

"I can't sleep," she said.

"What's the matter?"

"You know what's the matter. I'm afraid of getting pregnant."

"Let me rub your back," I said.

I gave her a massage, and soon she was sound asleep. Then, I couldn't get to sleep, and I had a big day the next day. I did a trick that my grandfather had taught me and hypnotized myself to sleep. It usually worked, and I slept until morning. I woke up refreshed and noticed that Pat was already in the kitchen, making coffee.

"Good morning," I said.

"Good morning," she said. "Thanks for helping me get to sleep last night."

"My pleasure. Did you have sweet dreams?"

"I always have sweet dreams sleeping next to you."

"What's on the agenda for today?" I asked.

"I'm in the studio most of the day. I won't be able to have lunch with you. What are you doing?"

"I have two classes today. Then, I'm going to the library to do some research."

We drank our coffee, and I was thinking that maybe we could get away to the Adirondacks for the weekend before it got too cold.

"Do you want to go to the mountains this weekend?" I asked.

"That would be great. It'll be like a honeymoon."

"Let's not talk that way for a while," I said.

"Why not? You said you'd marry me."

"In the distant future."

"What? Why?" she exclaimed.

"I have a lot of school left, and I don't even know where I want to live," I said.

"What's that got to do with getting married?"

"Don't pressure me, and I don't want to talk about it now. I have to go," I said.

I went into the bedroom, and I got dressed without a shower.

I was out the door in less than ten minutes.

"Goodbye," I said, kissing her.

"Bye," she said angrily.

My first class was with Laura, and I hadn't finished reading *To the Lighthouse*. The discussion went pretty well, and I was able to contribute. I couldn't take my eyes off of Laura. After the class, I went up to her and asked her a question about the novel. She answered it with a warm smile, and I was in a daze. I went to my second class, but I couldn't concentrate; I kept thinking about Laura. I didn't know how to approach her since she was engaged, but I was definitely going to work on it. I felt guilty thinking that way, but I rationalized that I had only been going out with Pat for a short time. I went to the library and read some articles on Virginia Woolf. I went home exhausted and called Pat.

"Hi," she said.

"Are you still angry?" I asked.

"A little."

"Do you want me to come over later?" I asked.

"Not tonight. I'm tired."

"Do you still want to go to the lake tomorrow?" I asked.

"Sure," she said. "Call me in the morning." I took a nap and got up an hour later. I made myself a sandwich and read the rest of Virginia's novel. I loved it. It was my favorite novel. I went to bed early so we could get an early start the next day.

Chapter III

I slept well and took a long hot shower in the morning. I felt ready to go into the Adirondack mountains. I called Pat, and she was still sleeping.

"Wake up, sleepyhead," I said.

"I'm up now. I'll jump in the shower and be ready by the time you come over."

"I'll see you in a few," I said.

I packed a few things and drove over to her apartment. She was getting dressed, but I was glad she didn't spend much time putting on her makeup. In half an hour we were ready to leave.

"I'm on the pill," she announced.

"Good. Now I don't have to wear a condom."

"Do you want to have car sex?" she asked.

"Sure, but a little bit later. Let's get up into the mountains."

We drove for an hour and a half, until we entered the Adirondacks. The hills were majestic, but the leaves had already peaked out. The road wound around lakes and small mountains. I wasn't in the mood for sex, so we decided to rest until that night. The pine trees were so tall, and they lined both sides of the road.

"What did you talk about in theory the other day?" she asked.

"I was pointing out that language is in motion."

"Isn't everything in motion?"

"Definitely. But what are the consequences of saying that language is in motion?"

"I don't know," she said.

"Well, knowledge can't be solid," I said.

"Doesn't memory slow down language?" she said. "That's where our knowledge is, isn't it?"

"Yes, but knowledge always comes out of memory differently than when it goes in."

"So, a word never means the same thing twice," she said.

"Now, you've got it."

The sun came out from behind the clouds, and the view was spectacular. The car moved gracefully around the curves, and Pat had a pleasant look on her face. We drove for a long time until, finally, we arrived at our motel. It was not busy, and we easily found a place to park. The room was small and inexpensive, since it was out of season.

"I wish it were warm enough to go for a swim," she said.

"We can go canoeing tomorrow," I said.

"That'll be great."

We took a short nap and dressed casually for dinner. There was a small restaurant nearby, and it was decent enough. In those small towns, you never knew what you were going to get. We ordered pasta, figuring they couldn't mess that up. We drank coffee and talked for a while before the food came.

"I think I want to be a news anchor someday," Pat said.

"You could do that. You're beautiful. You have a good speaking voice, and you read well. You're smart enough to write your own copy, too."

"Thank you. I'm going to have to support you while you write." She laughed.

"Don't laugh. You probably will."

"I would support you for the rest of our lives if I had to."

"You're sweet," I said.

"I expect you're going to get published in a few years

anyway," she said.

"We'll see."

The food came, and it was pretty good. We ate a lot because we hadn't eaten much all day, and we made our way back to the motel. We were tired and decided not to make love. I had a restless sleep, but Pat slept through the night. In the morning, I got up early and made the coffee. Pat slept until eight and woke up in a good mood. We got in the shower and made love. It was intense. It was the best way to start a day. The weather seemed to cooperate that morning, and we dressed to go canoeing. First, we went to a nearby diner for breakfast, and we ate some eggs and home fries. Pat was very careful about what she ate. She didn't want to gain any weight. I ate a great deal and never gained any weight.

"If we make a lot of money, I want to have a camp on one of these lakes," Pat said.

"We'll have enough money one day," I said, "but I don't want you to become obsessed with money. There are other things that are more important."

"I know, but it's nice to be comfortable."

"We'll be fine, but I want you to think more about art," I said.

"I think about art. You know I read the classics."

"And being from New York, I know you went to a lot of museums," I said, "but you're getting into a field where money runs the show, and I am worried you're going to get swept up into it."

"Maybe I can do some writing like you," she said.

"That would be great, as long as you don't get too involved in pop culture."

"You're too serious. There's nothing wrong with pop

culture."

"I guess you're right," I said.

We finished eating and walked our way to the docks where the canoes were. We pushed off, and I decided I would steer. The lake was calm, and there was a warm breeze from the south. She and I were both strong paddlers, but we took our time and went slowly along the edge of the lake. The sun was out with some white puffy clouds. I watched her strong back as she pulled the paddle through the water. Her hair glistened in the sun, and the water sparkled with the reflection of the sun. We didn't speak but moved in unison. The canoe slid gently through the ripples on the water. Stroke after stroke, we moved gracefully along the edge of the lake. I steered for a while, watching her pull us through the water. The water twirled behind the paddles, and soon we decided to rest. We glided in the shadows of the trees and listened to the birds' sing. After an hour or so of canoeing, we went back to the launch.

"That was great," she said. "We'll have to do this again later."

"It's so relaxing on the lake," I said.

"I think I'll read outside of our room and enjoy the rest of the day," she said.

"Good idea," I said.

We went back to the motel and sat outside since it was such a warm day. I began reading another Woolf novel, and Pat read the rest of the evening. I wrote down some notes and thought about Virginia Woolf's tragic life. I knew that if she had lived fifty years later, they would have had medication for her and would have probably saved her life. We decided to go canoeing again as the sun was setting, but we followed a different path. Afterwards, we went back to the motel exhausted, and fell right to sleep. I slept through the night, but had a nightmare in the morning.

I dreamed that Pat and I were swimming in a lake, and that suddenly she pulled me down under the water. Then, Laura swam in and tried to pull me up. I was drowning when, suddenly, Pat let go, and I went to the surface with Laura. I took a deep breath and swam to shore next to Laura. I woke up in a sweat, taking a deep breath.

"What's the matter?" Pat said.

"I had a bad dream," I said.

"It's over with now," she said.

"Hold me," I said.

She held me, and we kissed. After a while, we decided to make love. It was intense. She lay on her stomach and kept her legs together as I entered her from behind. I lasted a long time, and I came inside her.

"Wow!" she said. "There's something about this mountain air that inspires you." She laughed.

"You're still using protection, aren't you?" I asked.

"Yes. Don't worry. I've been thinking about it. I don't want to have children for a long time."

"Good," I said.

We took a shower and got dressed, thinking that we would go for a walk along the lake. It was a cloudy day, but it was warm, and the birds were chirping up a storm. We walked in single file along the path as the twigs crackled under our feet. The air smelled great and the trees gave off a strong scent. She was wearing tight jeans and walked ahead, my eyes glued to her ass.

"I'd love to have a camp on this lake," she said.

"It would be good for my writing," I said.

I kept thinking about Laura even though I was with Pat, and

25

it made me feel uncomfortable. We took our shoes off at one point and stepped into the water, which was very cold. We held each other and kissed, and I imagined kissing Laura. I felt a pang of guilt and quickly brought myself back to Patricia.

"I'm warm on top and cold at my feet," she said, laughing.

"You'll be warm all over later," I said.

We walked some more along the lake, and the forest was alive with sounds. There was poetry in the forest, and I decided to write a poem later. She was happy, which made me feel good.

"How many children do you want to have?" she said.

"Maybe none. I don't know."

"We have to have two anyway," she said.

"Why are we talking about this now?" I asked.

"Because, we have to plan ahead. We can't not talk about it. Besides, I want to have them fairly early, so I can enjoy my forties and fifties without them."

We walked back to the motel and sat outside in our lounge chairs. It was peaceful, and nature always brought me back to my childhood. I had been a happy child, always involved in athletics, and I had spent quite a bit of time in summer camp. I could sense though that Pat was irritated with me, since I didn't want to make a commitment on children.

"Don't be upset with me, honey. I'm only twenty-six and you're twenty-four. We have a long way to go before discussing children," I said.

"I know, but I like to think about it. That's all."

"I like children, but my writing comes first. I have to put myself in a position where I can write every day. I don't think you understand that," I said.

"I understand, but lots of other writers have children."

"I know. I know."

"Well, you think about it, and we'll leave it alone for now," she said.

"Good idea," I said.

I was thinking about Laura, who didn't have children and probably didn't want any. She was a real professional, and I knew many intellectuals simply didn't have children. Many did, of course, and that was my dilemma.

We went to lunch at a little diner and had fresh salads with seafood. I loved seafood, and so did Pat. Even though she was very tall, she was a light eater and kept her shape nicely. I exercised most days and ate with a healthy appetite. The salads were good, and we talked about several different things.

"Why don't we invite your mom for dinner and tell her we're engaged," Pat said.

"That's a good idea," I said.

I thought with trepidation that I was getting myself more deeply involved, without wanting to. I really didn't want to get married, but I didn't know how to tell Pat. I wanted to marry Laura even though we hadn't even gone out on a date.

"I already told my mom," Pat said.

"What did she say?"

"She said congratulations."

"I don't think we should tell everybody right now," I said.

"Why not? You're not backing out on me, are you?" she said seriously.

"Not really, but I need to have more time to think about it."

"You piss me off," she said.

"Don't take it the wrong way. It's still new to me. That's all," I said.

"You're full of shit. You don't want to get married, much less have children."

"I didn't say that. Calm down."

"I'm going back to the motel," she said.

She stormed out and left me sitting there, embarrassed. I was glad, though, that I had said something. I couldn't get Laura out of my mind. I finished eating my salad and walked slowly back to the motel, not knowing what to anticipate. Pat was sitting outside, reading, and she pretended I wasn't even there. I went inside and lay on the bed face down. I felt horrible and wanted desperately to make up with Pat. I went outside and sat next to her quickly.

"I'm sorry," I said. "I don't think I'm ready to be engaged."

"Are you breaking up with me?" she asked.

"No. Of course not. I'm only taking a step back."

"Well, maybe we should spend some time apart so you can think about it," she said. "I want to go home right now."

"All right," I said.

We packed up our things and drove back to Syracuse. The drive was a long one, and hardly a word was spoken. I dropped her off and went back to my studio. I turned on the television and tried not to think. All I could think about was Laura. I wanted to look her up in the phone book, but I was afraid to bother her. I had called other professors to ask certain questions, but that was different. I decided to read and picked up *Orlando* by Virginia Woolf. I read for a long time and finally decided to call my mother.

"Hi. How are you?" she said.

"Not too good," I said. "Patricia broke up with me for a while."

"Did you have a big fight?" she said.

"Yeah. We were engaged, and then I broke it off."

"You're not ready to get married. She'll come around after a while. Leave her alone."

"Okay. I won't call her. I'll talk to you later. Thanks, Mom."

I ate something, then went back to reading. I couldn't concentrate on the book. I kept thinking about Pat and Laura. I was tempted to call Pat but resisted. Finally, I went to bed, miserable, and tossed and turned for two hours. I fell asleep and didn't wake up until ten o'clock. I ate some cereal and watched TV. I wanted to call Pat in the worst way but didn't. I spent the day reading and didn't call anybody. I was unhappy, and wallowed in my misery. I fantasized about Laura but still didn't feel good. I went to bed early and fell right to sleep. I dreamed that Pat and I were fighting, and I woke up in the middle of the night. I decided to call her.

"Hello?" she said, half asleep.

"Hi, honey," I said. "Sorry for calling in the middle of the night, but I had a bad dream about you and wanted to make sure you're all right."

"Of course, I'm all right, and I'm still not talking to you," she said and hung up.

Now, I was really upset and couldn't go back to sleep. I read for the entire night and got up at six. I made a pot of coffee and drank the whole thing. I had class two hours later and almost fell asleep during class. Afterwards, Laura asked me why I hadn't participated, and I told her I was having personal problems.

"We all have those," she said. "I want you to come to class more prepared. And get some sleep," she added with a wink.

"I will. I promise," I said.

I was deeply in love, and her wink made me feel better. I thought I was glad Pat had broken up with me. Now, I could pursue Laura. I was confused though, because as soon as I left Laura, I started thinking about Pat. I went home and went right to bed. I slept through my next two classes and woke up feeling much better. I made a sandwich and more coffee. As I was sitting there eating, I got a call. I fantasized that it was Laura but was relieved that it was Pat.

"Hi. I'm sorry I was so rude last night," she said.

"That's all right. I shouldn't have called at that hour."

"Listen. I've been thinking," she said. "We don't have to be engaged right now. I don't want to break up. I'd like to get back together again."

"That's fine with me," I said. "Do you want me to come over?"

"Yeah," she said.

I took a quick shower and went over to her place. As soon as I walked in the door, she grabbed me and started pulling my clothes off. I laughed. She was trying so hard.

"Slow down," I said.

"I can't resist you," she said.

"It's only been two days," I said.

"I hate being away from you," she said.

She pulled down my pants and started sucking me gently. She held my balls tenderly in her hands as she moved her mouth over my cock. I came right away, and she spit it out.

"Don't like the taste?" I asked.

"It's too salty."

"Why don't I watch you masturbate?" I suggested.

She masturbated while I watched, and she came pretty quickly.

"That wasn't what I had in mind, but it was still pretty good," she said.

"We'll make love in the morning," I said.

We watched TV for a while and had a simple dinner of tuna fish sandwiches. We went to bed early and slept all the way through the night.

Chapter IV

I always slept better next to her. I had trouble alone. When I woke up the next morning, I was in a good mood. I made some coffee and let her sleep a little longer. I made eggs and bacon and brought them to her in bed.

"Breakfast in bed!" she said.

"Don't get used to it," I said, "but you can return the favor anytime you want."

"What are we doing this morning?" she said.

"We're going to make love. Then, we're going to school."

"Sounds good to me," she said.

We made love in the shower, and I came in her mouth, which was my favorite pleasure. She spat it out though, and I laughed.

"Don't laugh!" she said. "I can do it."

"I'm sorry," I said.

We got dressed and went to class. I was in class with Laura again and completely forgot about Pat. After class, I talked to Laura for a minute.

"I'm depressed a little," she admitted.

"Why?"

"I get depressed a lot. I don't know what it is. Maybe I'm manic-depressive."

"I tend to get manic," I said. "I have an unusual amount of energy."

"I wish I were like that," she said. "How are things going with your girlfriend?"

"Pretty well. She wants to get married, but I'm not ready for that."

"I don't think I'm ready either."

"My mother says if you're not one hundred percent sure, don't do it," I said.

"A wise woman," Laura said.

I got excited thinking that she wasn't ready to get married. Now, I thought I had a chance.

"What is your mother like?" I asked.

"We don't get along. She's happy, and I'm not."

"I love my mother," I said.

"My father died about ten years ago, and now my mother is very self-indulgent," she said.

"I love my father, too," I said. "He had a temper, but now he's fine."

We walked to her office and sat down. She had a small lamp on her desk, which gave off a beautiful, subtle light.

"That's why I don't want to have children," she said. "I don't think I would be a good mother."

"But you're so great with your students. I think you'd be a very good mother," I said.

I wanted to be with her whether or not she wanted to have children. She was a poet and a good thinker, and she intrigued me. Pat was as sweet but not as intellectual.

"I don't think I have the patience to have kids anyway," she said. "I have my students and my career."

"Then why get married at all?" I asked.

"No. You're right, I guess, but I want to get married like everybody else. My fiancé already has three children, and he's pretty traditional."

"I'm not sure if I want to have children. All I know is that I want to write," I said.

"Me too. I'm going to have to cut this short. I have another class."

"See you tomorrow," I said.

I went back to my place to take a nap, and I fantasized about Laura. I felt guilty, but it didn't stop me from thinking about her. I slept for an hour and made a sandwich. Then, I went back to school. My next class was theory, and it was very interesting. We were talking about the existence of God and how Derrida believed that since language is partially blind, God doesn't exist. I pointed out that only the argument from evil can prove the non-existence of God, and that no "deconstructive" argument could prove such a thing. This led to a furious discussion, and the professor wisely guided us through it without imposing any position. I talked to him after class, and he agreed with me.

"If we can know that God doesn't exist, then why can't we know anything else?" I asked.

"That's a good argument," he said.

I was really pleased with myself and couldn't wait to tell Pat and Laura my discovery. I went home and started reading theory to improve my position. I got carried away and didn't stop until Pat called.

"Hi," I said. "I've been reading."

"Do you want to get together?" she said.

"Sure. I'll be over in a little while," I said.

I took a long shower and fantasized about having sex with Laura. I drove over to Pat's place and kept thinking about literary theory. I was obsessed with philosophy at that stage of my life, and it caused certain problems for me. When I got to Pat's house, she answered the door in her black underwear.

"I can see what's on your mind," I said.

"Are you interested?" she said.

"Of course."

We went into the bedroom, and I told her to leave her panties on. I played with her, and she lay there, enjoying my probing fingers. We made love slowly and tenderly, and afterwards we got into the shower. While we were soaping each other up, I imagined I was with Laura. I liked the fact that Laura had more experience with men. She was confident about her beauty and made my knees weak. After Pat and I showered, we read in the living room with some music.

"Do you think we'll still be together in five years?" Pat said.

"How do I know? I guess so," I said.

"I feel so uncertain these days. You seem distant. We don't make love the same way we used to. You don't call my name and talk to me in bed any more."

"I'm under a lot of stress in school. I'll try to be more loving," I said.

"I think we need to take a break," she said.

"Are you still angry at me?" I asked.

"I guess so, subconsciously."

I hesitated for a second and thought this might be my opportunity to pursue Laura.

"Maybe we do need to take a break," I said. "If you're angry with me, there's no sense in going on."

"Why don't you go home then," she said calmly. I walked out the door with a feeling of relief and freedom. I went home and took a sleeping pill, thinking that I wouldn't be able to sleep. I tossed and turned for a while, but then the pill kicked in, and I fell asleep. I slept through the night and couldn't remember any of my dreams in the morning. I was used to waking up next to Pat, so it felt strange getting up alone. I made some coffee and felt a sense of loneliness. Then, I thought about seeing Laura later that day, and I felt better. I decided to call my mother, which I always did whenever I was having love problems.

"Hi, kid. What's up?" she said.

"Pat broke up with me last night," I said. "It doesn't bother me too much, but I'm feeling awfully lonely."

"You have a lot of male friends. This is the time you have to rely on them. Another woman will come along soon."

"I'll spend some time with Greg. Thanks, Mom. I'll call you soon."

I decided to call Greg, who was also in graduate school.

"Hi, Paul. How are you doing?" he said.

"Not too well. Pat broke up with me."

"That's too bad. Did you get into a bad fight?"

"Why don't we have coffee this afternoon, and I'll tell you about it."

"I'll meet you at three," he said.

"Okay. Talk to you later."

I got ready for school and walked to class. I was taking a Victorian literature class and was reading *Wuthering Heights*. I went to that class and had to sit through a very boring lecture. Then, I went to Laura's class. I sat in the front so I could stare at her. She pretended I wasn't even there, and so I spoke up during the discussion. I made a point that Virginia Woolf was manic-depressive and thought about death more than normal people. This turned the discussion, and by the end of class, Laura was defending my position. I walked up to her after class and asked to speak to her.

"Sure. Come into my office," she said.

We walked down the corridor together, and I was conscious of other students watching us. I didn't really care, but the gossip around there was incredible. I sat down in her office and watched her gracefully putting her papers away.

"I'm bipolar myself," I said to her, "but I only go manic. I don't get depressed."

"I wish I didn't get depressed," she said, "but I don't get suicidal like Ms. Woolf."

"That's good. Do you get regular exercise? I know that helps," I said.

"I'm starting to run a little bit, and that does seem to help. I've got to lose the pounds."

"No. You look perfect," I said.

"Thanks. You're very sweet. Intellectuals are always worried about going crazy. It's an occupational hazard."

"I went off the deep end when I was nineteen," I said. "I was at Georgetown and was running for an hour a day, until I got so manic, I stopped sleeping at night."

"And you were hospitalized?" she asked.

"Yes, for two weeks until my meds were stabilized."

"I've never had a breakdown, but I've been close, I think," she said.

"Fortunately, I recovered one hundred percent," I said, "or I would never be able to be in graduate school."

"Yes, you're as sharp as a tack," she said.

"Thank you. Well, I'd better be going."

I left feeling elated. I was in love, no matter what she said. It was blind love, certainly the best kind. I went to the coffee shop and waited for Greg. He showed up half an hour later, and I bought him a cappuccino.

"How are you doing?" he said.

"I'm in love," I said.

"I thought you broke up," he said.

"I'm in love with Laura, my Modern Lit professor."

"I know her. I thought she was engaged," he said.

"She is, but we've been talking and not just about literature."

"Are you sure it's not a rebound?"

"Who cares if it is. I'm still infatuated. Besides, how else am I going to get an A in the class?"

"She is beautiful, and probably too smart for you. But what do you care?"

"Apparently, she gets depressed a lot, which concerns me, but I don't really notice it when we're spending time together," I said.

"You'd better be careful. It's no fun living with a depressed person. I know firsthand," he said. "My first girlfriend in high school was always depressed, but she never let on, until one night she tried to kill herself."

"What happened?" I asked.

"She tried taking a bottle of sleeping pills, but her mother found her in time."

"I certainly don't want that to happen with Laura, but she says she doesn't get suicidal."

"What about Pat? She's a happy person, isn't she?" he said.

"Yeah. She's pretty happy, but she doesn't make me laugh. Laura makes us laugh in class even though she's so serious one on one."

"A lot of people are pretty serious," Greg said, "but some of them are content with their lives."

"I couldn't feel content or happy without a sense of humor," I said.

"Neither could I, so you'd better think carefully about who you get together with."

I took a sip of coffee and looked out the window. Several students were walking by, and I noticed a few very good-looking women. I had dated many women in undergraduate school, but so far had only gone out with Pat the last year or so. I was maturing and was trying to find someone to settle down with.

"I'm so infatuated with Laura that I can't see straight. She is so smart," I said.

"You're too young to settle down anyway," he said. "You'd better concentrate on your work."

"I can't avoid women," I said.

"Besides, I've noticed you've lost a lot your humor since you've been with Pat," he said.

"I know. I don't feel like my old self. I'll think about what you said. I have to go home and take a nap before I start studying."

"See you later," Greg said.

Greg always had great insight into my problems, and I usually listened to him, but I wasn't going to give up on Laura. I went home and tried to take a nap, but I couldn't sleep. I wanted to call Pat, thinking she would respond in some positive way, but then I thought better of it. I read for a while, and that put me to sleep. I had an odd dream. I dreamed that Laura and I were on a train, going through a tunnel, and she reached over and kissed me. Then, the train derailed. I woke up with a start and laughed to myself. I decided to call Pat, no matter what the consequences.

"Hi," she said. "What's up?"

"Nothing. I called because I miss you," I said.

"I miss you a little, too, but I'm not getting back together with you."

"I think we should have lunch sometime and talk things out," I said.

"Not yet. I have to get over you."

"I hope you'll never get over me," I said. "I don't think I'll ever get over you."

"I love you, Paul, but you have a fear of commitment. I need somebody who is going to be with me for the rest of my life."

I decided to cut the conversation short and thought about Laura.

"Okay. I'll talk to you soon," I said.

"Bye," she said.

Chapter V

I cooked myself some dinner and ate alone while reading. I was captivated by Virginia Woolf and kept associating her with Laura. Virginia's writing was very graceful, like Laura's movements. I read late into the night and fell asleep exhausted. I woke up in the middle of the night, and my first thought was about Pat. I was used to sleeping with her, and I missed her comforting me late at night. I thought about calling her but thought better of it. I tried going back to sleep, but couldn't. I kept thinking about Laura and Pat, and decided that I would ask Laura out on a date. I finally went back to sleep, and I got up later than usual. I made some coffee and ate a peanut butter sandwich. I was not happy. After I drank two cups of coffee, I felt a little better and took a shower. I kept thinking about how I would ask Laura out. I went to school and sat quietly in my theory class. I decided I hated Paul de Man's writing. He had some interesting ideas, but he was a pessimist, and I hated negativity. I was an optimist no matter what.

When I got to Laura's class, I was very anxious. I had drunk too much coffee, and besides, she made me nervous.

"Hi," I said, as I walked past her desk.

"Hi, Paul. How are you?"

"Not great," I admitted.

"Why don't we talk after class," she said.

"Okay," I said.

I sat through the class, not saying anything, but listening carefully. We were talking about *The Years* by Virginia and how she removed history from the novel. I was fascinated. I wanted to write my second novel like the outside world didn't even exist. After class, I waited for everyone to leave, and I approached Laura.

"You didn't say anything today," she said.

"I have some personal problems I've been dealing with," I said.

"We all have those," she said. "What's the matter?"

"My girlfriend broke up with me."

"That's too bad," she said. "How long were you going out?"

"About a year. She wants to get married, and I'm not ready for it."

"You might be too young to get married," she said. "On the other hand, I got engaged when I was about your age."

"Why didn't you get married right away?" I asked.

"I told you. We're separated, and I've always been a little unsure, to tell you the truth."

"Is anyone ever completely certain?" asked.

"I don't know. I guess some people are, but things change over time. People grow apart."

"I think Pat and I have grown apart over the past year." I looked at her blue eyes and thought that I could never be more certain about my love for her. I wanted to play it cool, but I had butterflies in my stomach.

"Sometimes I think Robert is too old for me," she said, "but I like his maturity."

"I think I'm mature for my age," I said.

"Yes, you are. I matured late," she said.

"Would you like to have lunch with me sometime. I don't like to talk in these offices with thin walls," I said.

"Sure. Sometime next week would be fine."

"I'll see you soon," I said, feeling so nervous that I cut the conversation short.

I walked out and took a long breath. I thought she was in love with me, too. I walked home and didn't know what to do with myself. I turned on some music and sang along with the song. I thought about Pat and wanted to reconnect with her in case things didn't work out with Laura. I was impulsive and thought I could control everything. I decided to call her.

"What's up?" she said.

I didn't like the sound of her voice.

"You don't have to be like that. I thought you still loved me," I said.

"You know I love you, but I'm getting tired of your bullshit."

"I want us to get back together again," I said. "I can't live without you."

"That's exactly what I mean. You can't commit, Paul. You want to get back together. Then, a month from now you'll want out."

"This happens to all couples early on," I said. "We're still adjusting to each other."

"You have to settle down," she said angrily.

"Don't be angry. Doesn't it make you feel good that I love you?"

"I'm not angry, just frustrated," she said. "I miss you, too, but you break my heart. I want to marry you."

"I know, and we will get married someday, not right away is all."

"You want to fuck a bunch of little blondes. Don't you?" she said.

"Come on. You know that's not true," I said, thinking about Laura.

"Don't call me for a few days," she said.

"All right," I said, and hung up.

I was upset and made a pot of coffee. I had lot of reading to do, but knew I couldn't concentrate. I decided to call Greg.

"Hey, what's up?" he said.

"I'm a mess," I said.

"What's the matter now?"

"Same thing. Only it's getting more complicated. I have a date with Laura, but Pat still doesn't want to get back together."

"Maybe you should move on and concentrate on Laura," he said.

"I know, but what if Laura doesn't like me in the way that I like her, and I end up losing Pat?"

"You have to take a risk with Laura, I guess. It seems to me you've already lost Pat."

"No. Pat wants to marry me. I can't commit. That's why she's upset. I don't know why she's putting so much pressure on me."

"You should be glad that she loves you. She's beautiful and nice. I don't know why you don't want to marry her," he said.

"Because I'm also in love with Laura."

"You're impossible," he said.

"I know. I'm fucked up." I laughed.

"When's your date with Laura?"

"Sometime next week. Do you think she must really like me to go out for lunch?"

"Of course, she likes you. Don't doubt it. Be confident even if you're not."

"I feel guilty about Pat though. She doesn't deserve my going out on her behind her back."

"You can't feel too guilty. You're going to do it." He laughed.

"I'm a scoundrel," I said.

"You're young and foolish. That's all," he said. "I've got to go. Give me a call tomorrow."

I suddenly felt all alone. I looked up Laura's number in the phone book and found it. I wanted to call her in the worst way, but I was afraid to. I decided to call her with the pretense that I needed to talk about a novel.

"Hello?" she said.

"Hi, this is Paul. I have a question about class."

"Sure. What's the question?"

"Is the lighthouse in Woolf's novel a phallic symbol?" I asked.

"What do you think?" she said.

"I think it is."

"I agree with you," she said.

"I know that's an odd question, but I was curious," I said. "Actually, I called because I'm very upset about losing my girlfriend, and I needed somebody to talk to."

"That's all right. I know how you feel. I had a bad breakup once, and I couldn't let go."

"What happened exactly?" I asked.

"I was in my first year of graduate school, and he was getting his doctorate. We went out for about eight months. Then, he started cheating on me. I found out from my girlfriend. I confronted him, and he lied to me. Finally, he admitted to it, and I took him back. Two weeks later, he broke up with me. I kept calling him and writing letters, but he wouldn't respond. I was devastated."

"That sounds horrible. How long did it take you to get over him?" I asked.

"Almost a whole year, but I even think about him now

sometimes."

"You're a passionate woman."

"I'm too sensitive," she said.

"You can't be too sensitive."

"I think you can be," she said. "It's not good to take everything to heart."

"I guess you're right. You have to have a thick skin sometimes, and let things go. I guess I'm too sensitive, too."

"So was Virginia Woolf. That's why she was such a great writer," she said.

"Well, thanks. I feel much better now. I'll see you tomorrow," I said.

"Take care, Paul," she said.

I loved hearing her say my name. I finally settled down to read and, after two hours, fell asleep. I dreamed that I was making love to Laura, and I woke up with a smile on my face. I spent the rest of the evening cleaning my small apartment and thinking about the two women in my life. If only I could combine elements from each of them into one woman. I know that I preferred Laura though. She was more mature, and I enjoyed the challenge. I ate something late and read in bed until I fell asleep. I got a good night's sleep and woke up refreshed. I made some coffee and thought about calling Pat but didn't. I had a busy day ahead of me and was looking forward to it. I was going to theory class and then would stop in to see Laura. The days were getting cooler, and the leaves on the trees were turning a bright orange. I took a hot shower and drank two cups of coffee.

I walked to school and felt pretty good. I missed Pat but was excited to see Laura. I went to my theory class and participated quite vigorously. I pointed out that for de Man, one couldn't know the present. Then, why was the past unforgettable? You couldn't have it both ways. This led to a furious debate, which didn't end until the class was over. I was still in deep thought as I made my way to Laura's office. I knocked gently on her door and heard her soft voice.

"Come in," she said.

"Hi," I said.

"How are you feeling today?" she said.

"Better. I'm beginning to accept the fact that I'm really not in love with Pat."

"Why do you say that?" she asked.

"Wouldn't I have married her if I were in love with her?"

"I guess so, but it's not always that simple. You can be in love and not want to get married."

"She doesn't really have a great sense of humor, and that bothers me. We're always so serious."

"I know what you mean. My boyfriend is very serious."

"I haven't been my jovial self since we started going out," I said.

"I try to bring some humor to class," Laura said.

"And you do a good job of it, too," I said." But Virginia Woolf didn't have much humor in her novels, did she?"

"No. She was pretty dark, but she had moments of joy and contentment."

"And moments of sensuality," I said.

"She was very delicate and graceful," Laura said.

I was mesmerized by her smiling face. She had such a sweet way about her.

"What do you like about your boyfriend?" I asked.

"He's smart and very gentle, and he loves me."

I wanted to ask her what she liked about me, but I didn't have the courage.

"You could have had any man you wanted," I said.

"I don't think I've met the right man yet," she said, "though I'll probably marry my boyfriend anyway."

"Why get married if you don't think he's the right one?"

"I'm getting older," she said.

"You're not that old."

"Thanks, Paul. You're sweet."

"I have to go. I'll talk to you soon," I said.

I realized that I had left abruptly, but I wanted to leave on a positive note. I felt like we were getting closer, but I was very afraid to make a real move. Now, I was worried that she was going to marry her boyfriend. I knew I had a small chance to pull her away. I was trying hard to be witty, like I was in class, but I wasn't doing well with it. I walked home slowly, thinking about my theory class as well as Laura and Pat. I wanted to get laid, but I figured it wasn't going to happen for a while. As soon as I got home, I decided to call Pat.

"Hi," she said.

"I miss you," I said.

"I miss you, too."

"Really? I'm surprised," I said.

"Why are you surprised? You know I love you."

"Yeah, but I can tell by your tone that you're still upset with me."

"Of course. That hasn't changed."

"I want to see you," I said.

"Come on over late tonight," she said, and hung up.

I was relieved and pleased. I tried to work for a while, but I was too excited to see Pat. I took a long shower and watched TV for a few hours. I wasn't paying attention and realized at ten o'clock that it was time to leave. When she opened the door, she was wearing a black negligée.

"Wow!" I said.

"You like?" she said.

"You look great!"

"Not as good as that professor of yours."

"Who?"

"I hear her name is Laura," she said. "People talk, you know."

"I'm not interested in her. I ask her questions about class."

"Sure. That's all right. I'm interested in someone else, too," she said.

"No, you're not, are you?"

"He's a guy in my production class."

"Then, you've known him for a while," I said.

"Yup."

"Well, nothing is going on between me and Laura."

"Nothing is going on with me either," she said.

"Then why did you bring it up?"

"Because now I don't trust you."

I didn't know what to say. I wanted to say that she could trust me, but I couldn't bring myself to do it. I wanted to sleep with her, so I knew I had to resolve this somehow.

"That hurts my feelings," I said.

"You hurt mine, too, Paul."

"I'm sorry. I really am," I said.

"Do you want a soda or something?" she said.

"How about some tea?" I asked her.

"That'll be good."

I felt better immediately. She was a forgiving person, and I really did love her. I thought about Laura and felt guilty. I made some tea, and we sat in the kitchen, listening to music.

I watched her as she lifted the teabag up and down gently.

Her delicate hands were so graceful. She had long, thin fingers. The tea was hot, and I watched the steam float up while I looked at her. I sipped the tea slowly and kept my eyes on her. She smiled as she drank her tea and looked right into my eyes. We were silent for a long time, her hands wrapped around the cup, and my lips sipping gently.

"I know you're lying," she finally said. "I can always tell with you. You're so honest."

"If I'm so honest, how can I be lying?"

"Usually, you're honest, but you lie from time to time, and I know you're lying now."

"I want to make love to you," I said.

"Now you're telling the truth," she said. "See, I know you."

"Can we?" I asked.

"Of course. You don't think I'm going to let this professor steal you away, do you?"

I leaned over the table and kissed her. She had such tender lips. We walked in the bedroom, holding hands, and she put a cloth over the lamp.

"Leave your panties on," I said.

"Okay."

I took my clothes off and watched her take hers off. We got on the bed and kissed for a while, rubbing each other's asses. I was hard already, and she stroked me gently with her hand. I sucked on her nipples, and made my way down to her black panties. I pulled down her panties and sucked on her pussy slowly and softly. She moaned, and I licked her in circles, inserting my finger. I did this for a long time, until she came. I got on top of her with her ass facing me, and we moved in unison, slowly, rhythmically. She came again, and then I came, thrusting deep inside her.

We rolled over exhausted, and we both had smiles on our faces.

"That was great," she said.

"You are so sexy," I said.

"I bet I'm sexier than your professor."

"Oh, don't start that."

"You're never going to find somebody that loves you more than I do," she said.

"I know that. Come on. Let's take a shower and go to bed."

We got in the shower, and she soaped me up, which felt so good. After our shower, we went to bed and fell asleep in each other's arms. I slept better when I was with her, but I couldn't stop thinking about Laura. I dreamed that Laura and I were hiking in the Alps, and that I ended up breaking my legs. When I woke up, I thought it was funny, but I felt worried.

I got up early and made some coffee. I felt great, having been laid the night before. Pat got up a little while later and came out in her underwear.

"Do you want to have sex this morning?" she said.

"You're insatiable," I said.

"We used to do it three times a day."

"I have to go to class," I said.

"Suit yourself. I'm sure you can do it under the teacher's desk."

"Sarcasm doesn't become you," I said.

We drank our coffee in silence, and I felt like she had ruined the morning for me. I had been looking forward to seeing Laura, but now I felt bitter. It occurred to me that sarcasm was a bitter sense of humor that was very negative. Pat wasn't usually sarcastic, but sometimes it slipped out.

"I'm not interested in my professor," I said. "Besides, she's engaged."

"Really? To whom?"

"A professor at Yale."

"That's funny, a triangle of students and teachers," she said.

"It's only the two of them. I'm going. Do you want to get together later?"

"I don't think so," she said.

"Okay," I said, and left.

Now I was pissed, and I thought about Laura all the way to school. I knew it was my own fault that Pat was upset with me, but I still blamed her. I thought about breaking it off with Pat for good, but decided I'd better cool off before any big decisions. I got to school early and went directly to Laura's office. I knocked and heard her say: "Come in."

"Hi," I said. "I need to talk to you."

"You sound troubled," she said.

"My girlfriend really pisses me off."

"What happened now?"

"Somebody told her I was having a relationship with you, and now she's jealous and doesn't trust me."

"That's interesting," she smiled.

I liked her smile and the way she responded. It was as if we really were having a relationship. At this point, I felt I could tell her almost anything.

"I don't know if I should break it off with her, or keep going," I said.

"Don't make any rash decisions. Give yourself some space and think about it. You can always talk to me."

"I'm so grateful to you for listening to me. Sometimes I feel like I can't talk to anybody," I said.

"I know how you feel. Everybody is caught up in their own stuff."

"Do you want to have lunch with me today?" I asked.

"Sure. You pick the place."

"I'll meet you at David's at twelve," I said.

"Fine. See you then."

I was elated and almost tripped walking out of the office. I went to my theory class and didn't hear a word that was said. After class, I had an hour to kill, so I went to the library and read over some of *To the Lighthouse*. I kept fantasizing about Laura, and I tried to imagine being married to her with children. As I made my way to the restaurant, I told myself to calm down. She was already there, waiting for me.

"Hi," she said.

"Hi," I said, not knowing how else to greet her.

"I brought a poem for you to read," she said.

"Isn't that thoughtful!" I said.

I sat down, ordered a cup of coffee, and read the poem. It was great.

"Fantastic!" I said.

"Thanks," she said. "I wrote that about two months ago, when I was feeling good."

"It shows optimism and strength," I said.

"I rarely write like that. Most of my work is pretty dark."

"I write optimistically," I said, "except my novel has a tragic ending."

"How can tragedy be optimistic?"

"It depends on how the characters respond to the tragedy. In this case, the girlfriend is very sad her boyfriend died, but knows he loved her. She feels renewed in her efforts to find love again."

"Very interesting," she said.

The coffee came, and we ordered lunch. I was looking at Laura's hands as she sipped her coffee. She had delicate fingers, and she wrapped them completely around the cup. She lifted the cup slowly to her lips and took very small sips. At times, a drop of coffee would hang on her lips and she would lick it off.

"When are you going to give me your novel to read?" she said.

"I'll bring it to the office later and put it in your mailbox."

"I'll read it tonight," she said.

"In one night?"

"Sure."

"I read very slowly," I said, "but carefully."

"You read theory. That's why you read slowly."

Our lunches came, and we were silent for a while. I couldn't take my eyes off her. She ate small bites and chewed slowly. She had sensuous lips, and I watched them as she ate.

"Do you dance?" I asked.

"Sometimes," she said, "but only after a couple glasses of wine."

"I'm a good dancer," I said. "Maybe we could go dancing sometime."

"Maybe," she said simply.

There was hope. I could tell by the way she was smiling at me that she was flirting. I felt very immature with her, but I had a little confidence. I imagined having a bottle of wine with her and making love afterwards.

"Do you like to hike?" I asked.

"Sure. I go to the Adirondacks sometimes."

"I know a nice place where we can hike," I said.

"That would be great. I'll bring the wine."

I was excited and could hardly keep my cool. I watched her

hold her fork as she ate and imagined her kissing me. I thought about Pat for a second, but then I put her out of my mind.

"This Saturday is supposed to be warm. Maybe we could go then," I said.

"Fine," she said.

We finished eating, and I insisted on paying the bill though she wanted to pay half. We walked back to her office, and I left feeling great. I went home and put on some music, fantasizing the whole time about Laura. I studied for a while, then called Greg.

"Hey," he said. "How are you?"

"I'm great. I had lunch with Laura, and we're going for a hike on Saturday."

"Looks like you're going to get an A in that class after all," he said.

"Maybe a B. It depends on my performance."

"How was lunch? What did you talk about?" he asked.

We didn't talk about work. That's for sure. I asked her if she liked to dance or go hiking. That's about it. She likes to drink a little wine. I found that out."

"She sounds like she really likes you."

"I know. I can't believe it. I never thought I could get anywhere with her. I also told her I was ready to break up with Pat."

"I hope it works out for you," he said, "but I think you're taking too big a risk."

"I'm not in love with Pat. Laura interests me so much more."

"You used to be in love with Pat. What happened?"

"I don't know. Feelings change. I think it was mostly lust."

"Are you sure you're not just lusting after Laura, too?"

"Of course not," I said. "There's that element as well

though."

"I must admit that I'm a little jealous," he said.

"You won't be single too much longer," I said.

"I'm not really worried about it."

"Well, I'm going to go. I'll talk to you later," I said.

"Bye," he said.

I decided to drop off the novel in Laura's mailbox, but I didn't want to run into her. I wanted her to read it before I spoke to her again. She wasn't in the office, so I left feeling good. I went home and made a sandwich. I didn't eat very well when I wasn't with Pat. I turned on the TV and read at the same time. I imagined Laura reading my novel, but I wasn't sure if she would like it. It was bit too philosophical, and the story didn't really take off until the second half. I wanted to call Pat because I felt lonely, but I didn't at first. I read for a long time, and then I called her.

"Hi," she said.

"Are you still pissed?" I said.

"I can't stay mad at you long. You're too cute."

Thanks. You're cute, too."

"But I'm not thrilled with you either," she said.

"What's the matter now?"

"You're difficult to handle," she said. "One minute you want to get married. The next minute you don't. I don't think you're really in love with me."

"Stop. Of course, I'm in love with you, but you can't blame me for hesitating on marriage. I'm still young."

"You're not that young," she said. "I'm two years younger than you, and I'm sure about marriage."

"I have a lot of schooling left. We've been through this before. I don't want to argue."

"I don't want to argue either," she said.

"Do you want me to come over?" I pleaded.

"Sure. I'll make a quick dinner."

I took a shower and dressed. Driving over to her place, I imagined making love to her. I thought about Laura as well, and the two were starting to blend together. When I got there, Pat was stir-frying some chicken and vegetables.

"How are you, sweetheart?" I asked.

"Hungry," she said.

"Me too," I said, rolling my eyes.

We sat right down to eat, and the food was delicious.

"How was your professor today?" she said.

"She seemed all right. I didn't ask her."

"Sure. You probably went to her office to talk to her," she said.

"Now, you're imagining things."

"You've been different with me the last few weeks. I'm not imagining anything."

I ate quietly, trying not to get into a fight with her. She was starting to get worked up, and I feared the night would end in disaster. I sipped my coffee and watched Pat eat. She would open her mouth wide and slowly insert the fork. Then, she would pull it out with her lips tight against the fork. She was sensuous in everything she did.

"I brought a book with me," I said.

"I thought we would watch a movie and cuddle," she said.

"We can do both. I have a ton of work to do."

"I bet your professor is working you overtime," she said.

"Enough of that," I said evenly.

We finished eating, and I did the dishes. I thought about Laura while I washed the dishes, and I wondered what kind of food she cooked for herself. Pat rubbed my neck while I bent over the sink.

"That feels so good," I said.

"I want to make love," she said.

"We will," I said.

After the kitchen was clean, we sat in front of the TV and watched Fellini's *City of Women*. We both liked the movie and had watched it more than once. After the movie, I tried to read while Pat attacked me. I gave up, and we went into the bedroom. We made love slowly for a long time. She was on birth control, so I came inside her. I had an undeniable passion for her, and when we made love, I felt in love. Afterwards, though, I thought about Laura.

"That was great!" I said.

"I like it when we go slowly," she said.

"Did you come?" I asked.

"No. Close though."

"Why do you have such a hard time?" I said.

"Childhood trauma." She laughed.

"No. I'm serious. It makes me feel inadequate."

"You're a good lover. It's hard for me. That's all," she said.

"Maybe you could touch yourself when I'm doing it from behind," I said.

"I'll try it next time. Don't worry about it. I'm fine."

"Okay. We'll figure it out," I said.

We took a shower and got into bed. We both slept well, and I got up early, feeling refreshed. I got out of bed, trying not to disturb Pat, and went into the kitchen to make some coffee. The sun was shining, and it brightened the kitchen. Pat got up a little while later, and I poured her a cup of coffee.

"Thanks," she said. "How did you sleep?"

"I slept really well and had a nice dream in the morning.

What about you?"

"Me too," she said. "I have to go to the studio today. What about you?"

"I have to go to the library and do some research," I said.

I made some oatmeal, and we ate in silence. I thought about going to Laura's office but wasn't sure if I had the courage to do it. I didn't want to pester Laura, but I wanted to show consistent interest. We showered and dressed for school. I kissed her goodbye, and we finally departed on good terms.

The sun was still out as I arrived at the library, and I sat in a small room by myself, doing research. After two hours, I decided I had had enough and went looking for Laura. I found her reading in her office.

"Hi!" she said.

"Hi, yourself," I said, as calmly as I could.

"What's new?" she said.

"Can we still get away on Saturday?" I asked.

"Sure. I don't see why not. You seem more serious today. What's happened?"

"I made up with my girlfriend for now."

"Well, that's good, isn't it?"

"I'm confused about my feelings," I said.

"Oh, I see."

"I really like you, Laura. I can't keep it to myself any more."

"I like you, too, Paul, and I'm glad it's out in the open."

"That's a great relief. There's nothing worse than unrequited feelings," I said. "Now, you know why I'm confused."

"I've been feeling confused lately, too," she said. "My fiancé said he was always worried I'd find somebody my own age, and now I have."

"I'm going to break up with my girlfriend."

"Do whatever you think is right."

I could tell by the way she sounded that she was happy. I was so thrilled, I could hardly contain myself. I decided I would leave since I had heard everything I could possibly have wanted to hear.

"I have to go, Laura. Can I call you sometime?"

"Sure," she said.

I walked out feeling great. I suddenly started thinking about what I would say to Patricia. I didn't want to hurt her feelings, but I knew that would be the result. I went home and took a cold shower. I couldn't remember ever having taken one. I called Greg to tell him what had happened.

"Hey," he said.

"You won't believe it," I said. "Laura said she had feelings for me, too."

"Good for you," he said. "Now what are you going to do about Pat?"

"I have to let her down easy, but I'm not going to say anything about Laura."

"What happens if you sleep with Laura, and the sex is not half as good as it is with Pat?"

"I'm not worried about it. I'm not in love with Laura for the sex. We have an intellectual connection."

"You have to stimulate the entire being, mind and body," he said.

"I'm sure the sex will be great," I said. "Besides, after a few years, we'll only be having sex once a month."

"You're more cynical than I thought," he said.

"More realistic," I said, "but our emotional and intellectual life will still be vibrant."

"I hope you're right, but I wouldn't break up with Pat yet."

"Maybe you're right. I'll have to think about it," I said.

"Well, I'm going to go. I'll talk to you soon."

"Bye," he said.

I thought carefully about not breaking up with Pat. Perhaps I could tell her that I needed some space. I decided to do some reading, but after half an hour, I realized I hadn't retained anything. I turned on the television and began rehearsing my conversation with Pat. Finally, I called her.

"Hi," she said.

"Hi, sweetheart. How are you?" I said.

"I'm fine. You sound strange."

"I think I need a break from our relationship," I said.

"It's the professor, isn't it?"

"No. I just need to concentrate on my work right now. I have three papers due in two weeks, and I need time."

"Fine," she said, and hung up.

As soon as she hung up, I regretted the conversation. Immediately, I thought about Laura and hoped it would work out with her. I had a feeling of dread that stayed with me for a long time. I made something to eat and put on some jazz. I felt lonely and began seriously questioning my breakup with Pat. Though I knew I was pressing my luck, I decided to call Laura. "Hello?" she said.

"Hi, Laura. It's Paul."

"Oh, hi. How are you?" she said.

"I'm fine, I think."

"What's the matter? You sound depressed," she said.

"I broke up with Pat."

"It must have been difficult."

"My heart really hurt when I said it. She didn't deserve it."

"Do you regret it now?" she said.

"Not really, but I hate hurting someone's feelings."

"I know what you mean," she said. "I was thinking of breaking it off with my boyfriend."

"I wish you would."

"Do you really?" she said wistfully.

"Of course, I do. I want to go out with you."

"I want to go out with you, too," she said.

My heart started beating very quickly. I thought about telling her that I loved her, but I didn't.

"Saturday is only two days away," I said. "Then we can spend some good time together."

"Call me Saturday morning," she said.

"I will," I said. "Bye."

"Bye," she said.

I felt so much better after talking to her. I thought about Pat and had a twinge of guilt and a feeling of sadness. The feeling of elation quickly overcame the sadness though, as I thought about being with Laura on Saturday. I stayed up late that night, reading different things without being able to concentrate. I tried to go to sleep, but I couldn't. I thought about Laura, naked, and in my arms. Finally, in the early morning, I fell asleep. I had a dream that I was in a field, making love to Laura, and Pat came out of the bushes with a knife, trying to stab me. I woke up startled, at about seven in the morning, and I couldn't get back to sleep though I was very tired.

Chapter VI

I dragged my ass out of bed and made some coffee. I was tired but happy. I decided to skip my classes that Friday and stay home to study. I took a long shower and closed my eyes, while the hot water poured over my head. I fantasized about taking a shower with Laura. I put on some music and began to study until a couple of hours later, when I fell asleep. I had a sexual dream about Laura, which was very satisfying. I felt better after waking up from my nap, and I decided to call Greg.

"Hey, what's up, playboy?" he said.

"Don't call me that. My love life has been on a rollercoaster," I said.

"Where's your sense of humor, boy?"

"I've lost it, I think."

"Cheer up. You're in love," he said.

"I feel good about Laura, but I feel terrible about Pat. I really hurt her."

"She'll get over it. We all get burned once in a while."

"I know I've been burned before," I said. "I don't know what I'll do if Laura rejects me."

"You'll get over it, too, but you never know, this might be the love of your life."

"I hope so."

"I've got to go," he said. "I'll talk to you soon."

Greg always helped me put things in perspective. I felt a little better about rejecting Pat. She would find somebody more suited to her needs. I read, and then I started writing a paper the rest of the day. I went to bed at eleven so I would be well rested for the next day. I couldn't sleep though, because I was so excited to see Laura. I finally fell asleep around two and got up at eight. I had my coffee and took a shower. Then, I called Laura.

"Hello?" she said.

"Hi. It's Paul."

"Hi. How are you?" she said.

"A little tired, but it's a beautiful day."

"Do you know where we're going?" she said.

"There's a nice ski hill we can climb, not too far from here, and I'll bring a bottle of wine. Shall I pick you up in an hour?"

"That would be great."

"Bye," I said.

I went to the liquor store and bought a good bottle of white wine with some cups. I was so excited I didn't even pay attention to my driving. I got to her house a little early, but she was ready. I had never seen her in jeans, but she looked great.

"Hi," I said.

"White wine. My favorite," she said.

I was nervous and hardly knew what to say.

"This is a really nice hill. We don't have to do any rigorous climbing. We can sit and talk and drink wine," I said.

"Sounds great."

I drove carefully and tried to remember the shortest way to the ski hill. We found our way in about half an hour and hadn't stopped talking the whole way. She sounded pretty cheerful, which made me feel good. We climbed up the hill only for five minutes, and we found a comfortable place to sit. I opened the wine and poured us some.

"There's nothing like sitting under the sun and sipping on some wine," she said.

"I really like you, Laura," I said, "everything about you."

"You're only infatuated. That'll wear off," she said.

"No, it won't. I've been infatuated with you for a long time," I said, as I took a sip of wine.

"I'm infatuated with you, too," she said, "but I remember when I felt the same way about my boyfriend, and it wore off."

"Feelings change, of course, but love can grow deeper with respect and admiration," I said.

"I guess you're right."

I leaned over slowly and kissed her on the lips. She responded by kissing me back. Our tongues melted together, and her mouth was so sweet. I pulled back for a second and took another sip of wine. Then I kissed her again. She bit my lower lip gently, and I pushed my tongue deep inside her mouth.

"You're a good kisser," she said.

"So are you."

We stopped kissing for a minute and drank some wine. I watched her holding the glass delicately in her hand and imagined her hand on me. We looked into each other's eyes, and I could see the love she had for me. I was ecstatic.

"I love you," I said.

"I love you, too," she said.

I kissed her again and put my hand on her breast. She started rubbing my leg, and I got hard.

"I want to run away with you," she said.

"Fine with me," I said. "Where do you want to go?"

"Italy. You can teach me Italian."

"I have cousins in Italy who would love to see us," I said, "and from there we could go all over Europe."

"Wouldn't that be great," she said, moving her hand on my cock. I unzipped my pants and pulled it out. She stroked it ever so gently, licking my ear.

"You're wonderful," I said.

"So are you."

"I was so afraid you weren't going to like me in a serious way," I said.

"I didn't know how strongly you felt," she said. "I was always so happy when you came to see me."

She started stroking me harder, and I came in her hand. I zipped up my pants and forgot about sex.

"You could teach in Europe," I said, "and after I get my degree, I could teach, too."

"You'd be a good teacher," she said.

"I would love to teach and write. That's my dream," I said.

"I put down the novel after the first half, but then I picked it up again and couldn't put it down," she said. "I think you have talent."

"Thanks. It means a lot coming from you."

"I've written some poetry that I want to show you," she said.

"I'm going to write you a poem," I said.

"You're sweet," she said.

We finished the bottle of wine, talked for another two hours, and then decided to go home. It had been the best day of my life, and I thought these days would never end. I had forgotten about Pat for the moment, but she would creep into my thoughts later. As we were driving home, I thought that I hadn't even noticed the beauty of our surroundings. I had been so involved with Laura that the real world had disappeared. If only I could capture that perception.

I dropped off Laura and drove home with a smile on my face. We had loved and laughed, and I was happy.

Chapter VII

When I got home, I suddenly felt very lonely. I wanted to call Laura or Pat, but I decided it was better to be alone and work. I started writing a paper but quickly became frustrated because I couldn't concentrate. I wanted to start another novel but didn't have the time. I decided to write Laura a poem. It was my first poem ever, and I was afraid it wouldn't turn out well. I worked on it, kept erasing and rewriting, and finally ended up with something that I liked. I wanted to call Laura and read it to her, but decided to wait. I decided instead to call my mother.

"Hello?" she answered.

"Hi, Mom. How are you?"

"I'm fine. What about you?"

"I'm in love with Laura, my professor," I said. "I spent the day with her, and we had the best time."

"Good. I'm glad you're feeling better. How did you let Pat down?" she said.

"Not too gracefully, I'm afraid," I said.

"What did you say?" she asked.

"I told her we needed to take a break, but she already knew about Laura."

"Don't break it off with Pat completely," she said. "She's been good to you."

"That's what Greg said, too. Thanks, Mom. I've got to go."

"Bye," she said.

I wanted to call Pat right away but was afraid to. I didn't want her to scream at me or hang up. I knew that she still loved me, but she was tired of my bullshit.

I decided to call her anyway.

"Hello?" she said.

"Hi, honey," I said.

"I thought you wanted to take a break," she said, sounding irritated.

"I want to take a little break, but I don't want to break it off with you forever."

"You want it both ways. You want the freedom to date your professor, and you want to hold on to me in case it doesn't work out. Why do you think I would put up with that?"

"That's not true. I need time to think and be alone. I still love you," I pleaded.

"I love you, too, but don't call me again until you break up with your professor."

"I'm sorry," I said. "I won't."

After I hung up, I felt horrible. I knew that I was wrong for calling her, but that didn't change my feelings. I tried to concentrate on Laura, but it didn't work. I still felt rejected by Pat. I wanted to call Laura, to make myself feel better, but held off. I thought then that the only way to calm my mind was to read. I sat on my couch and listened to music while reading. I made sure that I was concentrating on the book, and after an hour, I realized that I had calmed down. I was hoping that Laura was thinking about me. I looked at the poem again, and still found it acceptable. It wasn't great, but for a first try it was pretty good. I decided to call Laura.

"Hello?" she said.

"Hi," I said. "How are you?"

"I was just thinking about you," she said. "I had a wonderful day."

"I did, too," I said. "I wrote you a poem."

"Oh nice. Read it to me, would you?"

I read her the poem and was a little nervous about it.

"That's beautiful. Is that your first one?" she said.

"Yeah. I still don't know what I'm doing, but I'm learning."

"You're going to be a good poet one day," she said.

"Thanks," I said. "Have you thought about what you're going to say to your boyfriend?"

"I'm still thinking about it. He's going to be terribly upset, no matter what I say."

"My girlfriend was furious, but I said that I needed to take a break."

"I'm glad you told her that. I'm not as brave as you are."

"You have to say something sooner or later, don't you think?" I asked.

"Of course, but I want to put it as delicately as I can."

"I understand," I said. "Well, I'll let you go. I'll see you on Monday."

"Bye," she said.

I was slightly upset that she hadn't said anything to her boyfriend, but I tried to be understanding. After all, we had only been on one date. We had had a form of sex though, and there seemed to be a strong connection. Now, I wished that I hadn't said anything to Pat. I wanted to talk to somebody about my messy situation, so I called Greg.

"Hey," I said.

"What's up, player?" he said.

"You always give me a hard time," I said.

"You still haven't regained your sense of humor I see." He laughed.

"I guess not, but I am in love."

"That's great, but they usually go together," he said.

"I did laugh with Laura today, but the drama quickly returned in my head."

"How can you work with all this going on?" he said.

"With literature you sort of weave the drama in your life with the interpretations of novels."

"I don't," he said. "I take a concentrated look at the text, without drama."

"That's impossible. We always bring in our stuff to analysis."

"Maybe you're right, but that doesn't mean if your life is crazy, you're going to analyze novels better." He laughed.

"No. I know. I have to settle down here. My life is insane."

"Well, I'm going to go. Thanks for the call," he said.

"Bye," I said.

Greg always made me feel better. He could make me laugh when no one else could. He had settled me down a little, so I figured I would read for the rest of the night. Greg had a point of not being too crazy when trying to read and write. One had to concentrate. I kept thinking about Laura as I read Virginia's novels. There was a certain melancholy about Laura that reminded me of Virginia's style. I read late into the night and fell asleep with a book in my lap. I woke up in the middle of the night and went to bed. I woke up early and felt tired. It was Sunday, so I took it easy the whole day, napped, and did some more reading. I wanted to call Pat but remembered what she had said to me. I called my father and talked to him for a little while. He and my mother were my great motivators. I went to bed early and slept the whole night. I woke up feeling rested.

In the morning, I made some coffee and put on some music. I felt in love. I had Laura's class first thing in the morning, and I knew I had to play it cool. I couldn't let anybody know that we were dating. Rumors were already being spread. I walked into class and smiled at her, not saying anything. I sat in the back and listened carefully to the discussion. I wanted to contribute, but kept my mouth shut. I was afraid to talk, which really bothered me. Laura looked at me from time to time, expecting me to say something. After class, I simply walked out without looking at her. I felt foolish but wondered how I was going to handle her class in the future. I skipped my theory class and went home. I decided to call Laura's office and talk to her.

"Hello?" she said.

"Hi. It's Paul."

"Oh, hi. What was up with you today? You didn't say a word in class," she said.

"I know. I don't know what happened. I froze. I'll be fine though."

"I don't want you to feel awkward in class," she said.

"I'll get over it. I kept thinking about kissing you." I laughed.

"That's not all you were thinking!" she said.

"I have a perfectly clean mind."

"Sure, you do."

"I cleaned it this morning. That's why I couldn't concentrate in class," I said.

"Seriously, are you going to be all right?"

"Yeah, I'll be fine. I'll see you in a couple of days."

"Bye," she said.

That made me feel a lot better. She was sweet, and I felt like I had never felt before. I had been in love before, but this was different. I couldn't concentrate on anything. I was still afraid of losing Pat, because I had this uneasy feeling that my relationship with Laura wasn't going to last.

I thought about lying to Pat and telling her that I wasn't seeing Laura. Pat could always tell when I was lying though, and I didn't think I could get away with it. I called her anyway.

"Hello?" she said.

"Hi," I said.

"What now?" she said.

"I broke it off with my professor. We weren't really going out to begin with."

"I don't believe you. That was too quick," she said.

"Pat, I love you. We've been together a long time. I don't think I can live without you."

"Don't be so dramatic," she said. "I really don't think you're ready for a mature relationship."

"Who's ever ready for a serious relationship?"

"Some people are," she said. "That's not any kind of excuse."

"I'm pretty mature for my age. I'll mature more as time passes."

"I'm not sure I want to wait," she said. "Anyway, I have to go. Call me in a week or so."

"Okay. Bye," I said.

I was disappointed but immediately thought about Laura, which made me feel better. I didn't know why I felt like I had to hold onto Pat, but that's how I felt. I was glad Pat had said to call her in a week. At least she hadn't cut me off for good. I worked on a paper the rest of the evening and thought about Laura most of the time. I went to bed early, and tossed and turned for an hour before finally falling asleep. I had a series of bad dreams and woke up early in the morning, feeling exhausted. I didn't like sleeping alone, and I wondered when I would be able to spend some nights with Laura. My life was too crazy, and I knew that was the reason why I was having bad dreams. Even though I felt in love with Laura, I knew that I had completely lost my sense of humor. I didn't feel like my old self, and I wasn't happy about it. The problem was that I didn't know what to do about it.

I made some coffee that morning and put on some jazz to make myself feel better. I knew I would call Laura later but didn't think it would put me in a better mood. I decided to call my mother. She was retired from teaching and was always glad to hear from me.

"Hello?" she said.

"Hi, Mom," I said.

"What's the matter? You sound depressed," she said.

"I am. I had bad dreams last night."

"That's not like you. What's bothering you?" she asked.

"I'm not sure, but it could be the way I'm treating Patricia. I'm stringing her along, and she's mad at me."

"Then maybe you should break it off and let her go."

"I guess you're right," I said.

"If she really loves you, she'll be there for you in the future," she said.

"Okay. Thanks, Mom. You made me feel better."

Suddenly, thinking about leaving Pat, I felt very lonely. I was in love with Laura, but Pat and I had a history. I was not good at letting go, and I figured I had a week to think about what I was going to say to Pat. I didn't know if I could go a whole week without talking to her though. I decided to go to the library to make myself feel better. I took a long shower and put on some warm clothes. I wanted to go to Laura's office but made my way to the library. I only stayed in the library for half an hour before I decided to go see Laura. I knocked on her door, and she said," Come in," very softly. I walked in and saw her face light up. I was so pleased.

"Hi!" I said.

"Welcome!" she said. "What a pleasant surprise!"

"I couldn't wait two days to see you. I hope I'm not pestering you," I said.

"Not at all. I didn't want to wait that long either."

"I have a question to ask you. It's not personal or anything, just something that's been bothering me," I said.

"Shoot," she said.

"I seem to be really serious lately. I've lost my sense of humor, and I don't know how to get it back."

"You're asking the wrong person." She laughed. "I haven't had a sense of humor since I was a little girl."

"But we laughed on Saturday," I said, "though I haven't felt that way in a long time."

"I think the early stages of a romance are exciting and bring out the humor, but in the long run, we get into patterns, whether they are serious or humorous," she said.

"I think I've been in a very serious pattern with Pat," I said, "and I don't like it. I don't think I love her any more."

"Why do you think it would be different with me?"

"We have an intellectual connection," I said. "We meet at a different level."

"But it doesn't mean it's going to be humorous," she said.

"I guess you're right. I want to get my sense of humor back."

"Well, we can try," she said. "I'll tickle yours."

"I would like that," I said, "but for different reasons."

"I think a relationship should be primarily serious, with humor as a highlight," she said, "but not too serious."

"I think a relationship should be lighthearted with highlights of serious problem solving," I said.

"There's a way of seeing humor in problems, too, I think," she said.

I looked at her and saw a beautiful, thoughtful face. I wanted to kiss her in the worst way.

"Well, I'd better be going. You obviously have a lot of work to do," I said.

"Thanks for stopping by. I'll see you soon," she said.

I loved talking to her. Our conversations were always so interesting. I wanted to make love to her, but I was afraid to suggest it. I would have to take her out to dinner and go home with her afterwards. I felt more confident than ever, but there were always problems. I didn't know what she would do if her boyfriend found out about us. She had been with him a long time, and he would put up a fight. I decided to go home and study. Some philosopher had said to get involved with your work when you're having problems with love. I studied for two hours and got restless, so I called Greg.

"Hello?" he said.

"How much is therapy tonight?" I asked.

"For you, free," he said. "What's up?"

"I'm nervous about my relationship with Laura, and I think I ruined everything with Pat."

"Anything else?" He laughed.

"Seriously though, Pat doesn't trust me, and Laura hasn't said anything to her boyfriend yet."

"Do you blame Pat for not trusting you?" he said.

"No, of course not, but now I wonder if I should have stuck with her."

"You know what I suggested," he said, "but I guess we really never take anybody's advice."

"I take advice sometimes," I said.

"I'm not really in a position to give advice," said Greg, "but I think you should do everything in your power to regain trust with Pat."

"How do I do that when I'm going out with Laura?"

"I don't know, Paul. There must be a way."

"I'm not breaking up with Laura," I said.

"You're going to end up losing them both."

"I think things will work out with Laura."

"Then you don't need my advice," he said.

"No. I appreciate your input, Greg, but eventually I have to sort things out for myself."

"Call me when there's a new development," he said.

"All right. Bye," I said.

He was frustrated with me, and I could understand why. I couldn't make a decision, and decisions were being made for me. I had no control, and I hated being without control. I thought carefully about how I would approach Laura. I figured I'd better back off a little. I was getting too intense. As soon as I thought that, I wanted to call her. I couldn't stop thinking about her. I didn't like being home alone. I wanted to go over to Pat's and have dinner, or at least watch some TV with her. I knew if I called her though, she would probably yell at me. I took a hot bath and planned my strategy. I would call Pat in the morning and insist on having lunch with her. I knew she missed me, too. I worked on my paper after my bath and listened to music while I wrote. My thoughts about Virginia Woolf's novels were woven with my thoughts about Laura. I worked late into the night and actually got a lot of work done.

I slept pretty well that night and woke up later than usual. I took a long shower and made some coffee. I had some cereal and thought about what I would say to Pat. I figured that whatever I said, she wouldn't respond well. I called her at about ten o'clock, hoping she hadn't already gone to school.

"Hello?" she answered.

"Hi," I said.

"I asked you not to call me for a while," she said evenly.

"I feel all alone," I said. "I'm sorry, but I had to talk to you."

"It's all right," she said. "I feel alone, too."

"I miss you already," I said.

"Things not going well with your professor?"

"I told you that's over with."

"I don't believe you," she said.

"I'm not a liar," I said.

"Yes, you are."

"I don't want to get into a fight," I said. "Do you think we could get together?"

"I suppose so, but we're not having sex."

"I wasn't thinking about that," I said.

"See, you're lying again," she said. "Come on over."

I took a shower and dressed. I was thinking, while I showered, that I was cheating on Laura. I didn't care about the guilt. I was going to go out with Pat anyway. I thought about how to seduce her, while I drove over to her place. I figured it would be almost impossible to talk her into having sex, but I would try. When she opened the door, she was fully dressed.

"Hi," she said casually.

"Hi, yourself," I said.

"Come on in. I'm cooking," she said.

I walked into the kitchen. She was cooking stir fry. It smelled great.

"Wow!" I said. "This looks fantastic."

"Don't get used to it," she said.

"I love you," I said.

"Don't start," she said.

"What? I said 'I love you'. That's all."

"You're not getting me into bed," she said.

"I just appreciate that you're cooking for me," I said.

"Sure," she said.

"This is not going to be one of those difficult nights, is it?" I asked.

"No. I guess not. We'll have a nice dinner and watch some TV."

"Where am I spending the night?" I asked.

"Here, with me, but we're not having sex."

"I heard you the third time," I said.

She stirred the food as I sat at the kitchen table, and I thought about the pattern that I was in with her. It was definitely too serious, and I longed to be with Laura. Even though Laura was serious as well, there was a lighthearted feeling.

"I'm going to work on my paper tonight, in here, while you watch TV," I said.

"That's fine. I'll do some reading, too."

"I don't want you to be angry with me, sweetheart," I said.

"Well, you've been acting very strangely lately. It's hard not to be angry."

"I know. I'll do better," I said.

I was thinking that if I could get on her good side, then maybe, while we were in bed, I could talk her into having sex.

We ate and talked about trivial things. A lot of the excitement of our conversations had disappeared. I felt like the relationship was almost purely sexual. I wondered what Laura was doing. After dinner, I worked on my paper. Interpreting Woolf's work was like analyzing Laura, and I knew the paper wasn't going to be very good. Pat worked, too, and after two hours, we decided to turn in. Pat put on her sweats, and I wanted to sleep in the raw.

"Why didn't you bring pajamas?" she said.

"I didn't think I would be needing them," I said.

"Well, put some of my sweats on."

"It's going to be too hot," I said.

"Too bad," she said.

I put on her sweats and got into bed. I was still going to try something. She got into bed and turned off the light. She turned away from me, and I put my arm around her.

"Watch yourself, mister," she said.

"I'm not doing anything." I laughed.

I put my hand on her stomach and rubbed her gently. She didn't say anything, so I pushed my cock against her.

"Stop it," she said.

We lay there for a long time, without moving, and eventually she fell asleep. I rolled over and went to sleep. I was glad to be with her—I didn't feel lonely. I woke up in the middle of the night and was wide awake. I got up carefully without waking her, and went out to the kitchen to work on my paper. I wrote for about an hour, then I went back to bed. She woke up, as I slipped into bed, and gave me a nice tender kiss. I wanted to make love to her, but she wouldn't let me. In the late morning we got up and made some coffee. I felt like we were married, and it felt good in one way, but I wanted my freedom at the same time. This was a paradox that I would experience frequently.

"What are you doing today? You already missed your first class," she said.

"I'm going to my second class. Then, I'm going to work on my paper."

"Do you want to come back here?" she said.

"Yeah. I'd like to."

"That's fine," she said.

We showered together, then we left for class. I wanted to see Laura very badly. I was a little late for class, but Laura smiled at me when I arrived. I didn't say much during class, but I felt more comfortable. After class, I went up to Laura and said hello.

"How are you?" she said.

"I feel pretty good," I answered.

"You didn't say much during class," she said.

"I'm getting back into the swing of things."

"Are you writing any fiction now?" she said.

"No. I don't have time, or rather I can't concentrate on it right now. I'll probably have to wait until the summer."

"I wrote a poem for you," she said.

"Really? I'm thrilled. Do you have it here?"

"Yes. It's right here," she said, handing it to me.

I read it slowly, going over it twice, and was moved.

"It's wonderful," I said.

"I like it, too," she said.

I wanted to tell her that I loved her, but held back.

"I'm going to write you another one," I said.

"I would love that," she said.

"I like using nature as my backdrop and central metaphor," I said.

"I could do that more often," she said.

"Well, I have to go. I'm working on a paper," I said.

"Bye," she said.

The poem had had a sexual element to it that got me excited. I wanted to make love to her so badly. I went back to Pat's place and started doing more research for my paper. I worked for a couple of hours; then Pat showed up.

"Hi!" she said, giving me a big kiss.

"You're in a good mood," I said.

"I got an A on my presentation."

"Good for you!" I said.

"Now we can make love," she said.

"Great," I said.

We got in the shower and we kissed under the running water. Immediately, I was hard as a rock. She rubbed soap all over me, and then I soaped her up. I thought about Laura while we were in the shower. Pat leaned over, and I penetrated her from behind. I moved slowly at first, kissing her ear, and licking her neck. She started talking, which was unusual for her.

"Fuck me. Oh, that feels so good. Deeper, harder," she said.

"You like that, huh? Yeah, you like that," I said.

I moved faster and faster, thrusting as hard as I could. She came after a few minutes; then I came on her ass.

"That was fantastic," she said.

"I like it when you talk," I said.

"I like it, too," she said. "It really turns me on."

"That was the best sex we've ever had," I said.

"It was," she agreed. "We keep getting better with experience."

"I need a nap after that," I said.

We crawled into bed and cuddled. We talked for a while, then we fell asleep. An hour later, I woke up. I slipped out of bed and let Pat sleep some more. I went into the kitchen and made half a pot of coffee. I sat quietly thinking to myself, drinking coffee. I enjoyed my time alone, especially when Pat was near me. I thought about Laura again, but not quite as obsessively. I thought about the poem she had written me, and I decided to write her one. I didn't know if I should write it there, so I figured I would wait until I was home alone. I worked on my paper instead and realized my impressions of Laura were creeping into my analysis of the novels I was researching. I couldn't think of any way to avoid it, so I let it be. After a while, Pat woke up and joined me in the kitchen.

"How's it going?' she asked.

"Not that well, actually," I said.

"You're still thinking about our lovemaking." She laughed.

"I can feel the echoes of it," I said.

"I bet your professor is not as sexy as I am."

"Will you let that go? She doesn't mean anything to me."

"All right. I won't say another thing about her."

I worked on my paper for a while, and Pat sat next to me calmly, sipping her coffee. I loved having her next to me, doing nothing. We didn't have to be watching television or listening to music. We could simply sit together and just be. Why did I think I would be happier with Laura? I stared at the novel I was studying, and I started thinking about Laura. She was so delicate in her movements and expressions. The conversations between us never ended. I was so infatuated. I couldn't see anything negative.

"What would you like to eat?" Pat said.

"A hamburger is fine," I said. "I'll make the salad."

I made a nice salad, and she cooked. I wondered if Laura cooked well. I thought I should cook something for Laura sometime; maybe at my place we would end up having sex. After we ate, I worked on my paper some more, and Pat read while we listened to mellow jazz. It would have been a perfect evening if I weren't obsessed with thoughts of Laura.

Chapter VIII

We went to bed at about eleven o'clock and fell right to sleep. As usual, I woke up in the middle of the night and remembered my dream. I dreamed that Laura and I were eating dinner at a fancy restaurant and that Pat was our waitress. While we were talking, Pat poured hot coffee in my lap, and I got up screaming. Then, I woke up. I sat right up in bed and woke Patricia.

"What's the matter?" she said.

"I had a bad dream," I said.

"You're all right. Go back to sleep," she said.

It took me a long time to fall asleep again, and I could hear Pat's rhythmic breathing. She slept so much better than I did. Finally, I fell asleep and slept until morning. I had a pleasant dream that morning about having sex with Laura. When I got up, I let Pat sleep some more as usual and went into the kitchen to make some coffee. I sat at the table, sipping my coffee, and I read over the paper I was writing. I didn't like it, but I wasn't going to change it. Pat got up an hour later and sauntered into the kitchen.

"Did you get enough sleep?" she said.

"Not really, but I feel pretty good," I said.

"Why do you think you have trouble sleeping?" she said. "Guilty conscience?"

"Of course not. I have an active mind that is hard to shut down."

"Maybe you should take a sleeping pill."

"I'm going to look into that actually," I said. "I'm going to talk to my doctor."

"Good idea. You don't have to take one every night, only when you're having trouble sleeping."

"I like it when you take care of me like this," I said.

"I will always love you, even if we're not together," she said.

I thought about that for a long time. She was willing to love me unconditionally, something which only my family did for me.

"I will always love you, too," I said.

"Then why don't we get married?" she said.

"We probably will. I have to get through school first."

I thought immediately about Laura and felt guilty as hell.

I drank my coffee quietly and tried to compare the two women. They were both attractive to me physically, but there the similarities ended. Laura was more mature and intelligent, and Pat was more sensitive emotionally, as far as I could tell. I stopped comparing them for the moment, though the comparisons would return.

"I know you have to get through school. So do I. What does that matter?" she said.

"I'm not ready yet, and that's all I'm going to say about it. I'm not going to argue."

"I don't want to argue either."

"I'm going to shower and go to school," I said.

"I'm right behind you," she said.

I thought she was going to shower with me, but I waited a few minutes, and she didn't join me. I showered for only five minutes and dressed quickly. I was anxious to see Laura. As I was dressing, Pat got into the shower. I got a quick glimpse of her perfect body, which still excited me. I left a note that I would be back later and drove to school. I got to class on time and gave Laura a warm smile as I entered. I sat in the back and said very little. I wanted to say more but couldn't. After class, I talked to her.

"Hi," I said. "Class was very interesting as usual."

"You didn't say much again," she said.

"I'm sorry. I haven't got used to dating you and taking your class at the same time."

"Well, I hope you get used to it soon. It'll only be another few weeks."

"I'm listening though. I think you have some great insights," I said. "I was wondering if you would like to have dinner at my place."

"Sure. When?"

"How about tomorrow night, about six?"

"Great! Just give me the address and I'll be there," she said.

I wrote down my address and said goodbye. I was so nervous. I didn't know why I was still so nervous around her, but I was. I had told Pat that I would go back to her place, but I decided to go grocery shopping first. I bought some steaks for Laura and me, and other side dishes. I took the groceries home and took a long nap. After my nap, I called Pat and told her I would be right over. I took a quick shower and put on my jeans. I drove over, but I was thinking about Laura the whole time. I thought I would have sex with her for the first time. I imagined doing it in different positions and how I would try to impress her. When I got to Pat's house, I simply walked in and gave her a kiss.

"Hi, handsome," she said.

"You're in a good mood," I said.

"Why shouldn't I be?"

"No reason," I said, "but sometimes you're not so glad to see me."

"I've decided I'm not going to pressure you in any way, and let things happen naturally," she said.

"That's a good idea. I like that," I said.

"I thought you might. Do you want to work on your paper while I study?"

"Sure," I said.

I took out a couple of reference books that I had brought with me, and I started working on my paper. Every once in a while, I would look at Pat relaxed on the couch, reading. I asked myself why I couldn't simply live this way the rest of my life. Then, I thought about Laura. If only I could live this way with her. I didn't know what it would be like to live with Laura, and that was part of the attraction. Two hours later, we had sandwiches for dinner in front of the television. I still didn't like the way my paper was turning out, but I didn't really care. I was getting tired of all the work I was putting in. I wanted to relax on a beach with Laura. After watching a movie, we decided to go to bed.

"Do you want to make love?" I asked.

"Not really. I'm not in the mood," she said.

"Maybe I can put you in the mood," I said, grabbing her.

"Don't," she said. "I don't feel like it."

"Okay, suit yourself."

We went to bed, and I felt rejected. She had been in a good mood, and I was sure she would have wanted to have sex. But she turned me down, and I couldn't figure out why. She fell asleep, and I couldn't. I stared at the ceiling for half an hour or so, and then turned on my side. I wanted to touch her and see if she wanted to change her mind, but I didn't. After a while, I fell asleep. Suddenly, out of a deep sleep, I felt her hand on my leg, rubbing my thigh. I turned over and kissed her, gently sliding my tongue inside her mouth. She touched me and stroked me gently. We ended up making love for an hour, and I brought her to two orgasms. I was practicing for Laura.

"That was wonderful," she said.

"I haven't been that horny in a long time," I said.

"I think I'm usually hornier than you," she said.

"You might be. I was surprised when you turned me down earlier."

"I'm sorry. I had a bad feeling."

"That's all right. I'm not always the most sensitive person," I said.

"You're very sensitive actually," she said. "Now, let's go to sleep."

"Good night," I said.

I slept beautifully after that and couldn't remember my dreams in the morning. I got up early and felt like going for a run. I hadn't run in a long time, but I knew it would help me concentrate better on my work and sleep better. I didn't wake Pat and simply went for a run around the neighborhood. I was out of shape and felt pretty worn out by the time I finished. Pat was up when I returned. She laughed at me because I was so out of breath.

"You need to work out some more so you can last longer in bed," she said.

"That is where I work out," I said.

"Do you want to shower first?" she said.

"Yeah. I have to go to the library to work on this paper."

"I'm in the studio all day," she said.

"I think I'll stay home tonight and keep working there," I said.

"That's fine," she said.

My plan was really to go home and clean up before Laura came over. I showered quickly, kissed Pat, and drove home. I was not a good cook, but I knew how to cook steak, and everything else was premade. I cleaned the apartment for about an hour and washed some dishes that had been sitting there. After that, I had nothing to do, so I worked on my paper some more. I tried to think of all the things that water or the sea meant to Virginia Woolf. I came up with quite a few, but I didn't really know how to incorporate them into my paper. After two hours, I put the paper away and watched some television. I couldn't concentrate on the TV. I kept thinking about Laura. She showed up right on time and looked great in tight jeans.

"Hi," I said. "Welcome."

"Hi," she said, giving me a kiss on the lips.

"Frankly, I'm frustrated with my paper," I said, "but I don't want to talk about that."

"This is a cozy place," she said.

"That's a nice way of putting it," I said.

"Well, it's small, but all graduate students have small places. It's all yours. That's what counts."

"I thought I would start cooking. We can talk in the kitchen," I said.

She sat at the kitchen table while I cooked. I put potatoes in the microwave but didn't turn it on yet. I took out a spinach soufflé to cook after the potatoes and put the steaks on. She had a big smile on her face, which made me feel good.

"I had a horrible talk with my mother this afternoon," she said.

"Why? What about?"

"She lives in a dream world. She's always so happy, and she got upset when I told her how much money I was spending on therapy," Laura said, her smile now gone.

"It seems reasonable that if you need therapy, you have to pay for it," I said.

"She's the reason I need therapy to begin with."

"My mother is great," I said. "She raised three boys by herself, and we all turned out well."

"But your father came back into the picture, right?" she said.

"Yeah. He's great, too."

"I wish my father were still alive," she said.

"Do you think that's why you're going out with an older man?"

"I think so, but I'm also attracted to you." She smiled.

"I'm in love with you," I said, getting over my fear.

"I think I love you, too," she said.

After the food was ready, we sat down in the kitchen and ate. The steaks were delicious, and so was the soufflé.

"You're a good cook," she said.

"This is about all I can do," I said.

I watched her eat, and she had a healthy appetite. I always ate quickly and was finished before her.

"Take your time," I said.

"You boys must have had to compete for your dinner." She laughed.

"There was never enough," I said. "Do you cook for yourself regularly?"

"I get takeout a lot," she said.

After she finished eating, I put the dishes in the sink, and we went into the living room. We continued to listen to music and sat closely together on the couch.

"I feel like I can trust you," she said.

"I trust you, too," I said, putting my arm around her shoulders. "I want to make love to you."

"Not yet," she said. "I'm not prepared emotionally."

"I understand. Take as much time as you need."

"I'm still dealing with my boyfriend," she said.

"What's going on with that?" I asked.

"Well, now that he knows about you, he's trying to win me back."

"I don't blame him."

"No, but it makes for difficult conversation," she said. "He's always on the defensive. We don't talk like we used to."

"That's too bad."

I kissed her, and she kissed me back. We made out for a long time until I put my hand on her breast. She pushed it away.

"Not tonight," she whispered.

"That's fine," I said.

"But let's keep kissing. I'm so wet," she said.

I was enjoying myself. I didn't really care if we had sex. I could wait. I was so excited that she implied we would be doing it in the future. She was a great kisser. She let me grab her ass for a minute, but then she pushed me away.

"I'd like to stay longer, but I have a lot of work to do," she said.

"That's all right. I'll see you tomorrow," I said.

After she left, I called Pat, since I was sure she was expecting it.

"Hello?" she said.

"Hi, sweetheart," I said.

"What's going on?" she said. "I miss you."

"Want me to come over?" I asked.

"Sure," she said.

I couldn't help but think about sex all the way over to her house. I felt guilty, but I didn't let it bother me enough, to be honest. When I got there, she gave me a big kiss.

"Hi, sweetheart," I said.

"I bought some ice cream. I thought we could have some while we watch a movie," she said.

"Great idea," I said.

We sat on the couch, and soon we were kissing passionately. She chewed on my lower lip, while I moved my hand down her jeans. I couldn't stop thinking about Laura while I made love to Pat. The next thing you know, we were naked and fucking our brains out on the couch. It was great as usual, and we kissed for a while afterwards.

"That was intense," she said.

"I don't know what came over me," I said.

"Keep jogging." She laughed.

We took a shower, and I felt like two women loved me. I thought about Laura while I was with Pat, but I really couldn't compare the two, though I tried. They were very different in some ways and similar in others, but when I was with Laura, I thought about Pat, and vice versa. After our shower, I sat down to work on a new paper for my theory class. Pat did some reading, and after two hours, we went to bed. It took me a long time to get to sleep, and I thought about seeing Laura the next day in class. Finally, I fell asleep. I woke up in the middle of the night after a disturbing dream.

In the dream, I was camping with Pat on a lake in the mountains. We were swimming in the lake on a sunny afternoon. Everything was perfect. I swam far out into the lake, and Pat followed me. Suddenly, Pat grabbed me by the legs and pulled me under water. I struggled and managed to escape her grasp. I swam ashore where Laura was waiting for me. I thought I was safe in Laura's arms, but she pushed me back into the water. I tried to get out again, but she continued to push me back in. Then, I woke up. I lay there with my eyes wide open and didn't wake

Pat. I tried to go back to sleep, but it took me a long time. I thought about the dream and figured it was due to my fear of losing both women. When I woke up in the morning, I felt irritated, and I reflected on my poor night's sleep. Pat stayed in bed, while I got up to make the coffee. I felt better after my first cup and decided to get Pat out of bed.

"Come on, honey. You can't stay in bed all day," I said.

"Half an hour more," she pleaded.

"All right," I said.

I went back into the kitchen and read a little, while I sipped my coffee. I thought about seeing Laura in a few hours and got excited. I was still in the infatuation phase with her, but I knew it would eventually wear off. Pat got up a little later and poured herself a cup of coffee.

"How did you sleep?" she said.

"Not too well," I said.

"You need to see your doctor," she said.

"Yeah. I will."

"I dreamed about you," she said.

"Really? What was it about?" I asked.

"We were driving through the mountains, and you kept swerving off the road. Finally, we hit a tree, but neither of us got hurt." She laughed.

"That's interesting," I said.

"What do you think it means?" she said.

"I don't know. It could mean a number of things, I guess."

"Could it mean you're reckless or irresponsible, but not enough to hurt the relationship?"

"It could mean that, but it could also mean that I'm not a very good driver." I laughed.

"I'll choose my interpretation," she said.

"I'll think about it some more," I said.

I took a shower and left for school. I told Pat I would be back later. I went to Laura's class and gave her a big smile when I walked in.

"Hi," she said.

I nodded and walked to the back of the class. I didn't say a word the entire class. Afterwards, I walked up to her desk and smiled.

"You were quiet again," she said.

"I'm sorry, but I feel like I'm going to blurt out something stupid."

"That's ridiculous."

"I have to go, but I'll call you later," I said.

"Take it easy," she said.

I didn't have to leave but felt afraid to talk to her. I went to my theory class and didn't say a word again, because I was analyzing why I was so afraid to talk to Laura. I felt confident around her sometimes, but at other times, I felt petrified. After class, I drove back to Pat's place and took a nap. Pat was out. She was in the studio that day. I slept for a long time and didn't wake up until Pat came home.

"Hi, sleepyhead," she said.

"What time is it?" I asked.

"Four thirty."

"Wow! I slept a long time," I said.

"Well, if you're not sleeping at night, you're going to end up sleeping in the afternoon. Then you'll have trouble the next night. It's a cycle," she said.

"You're right."

"How was class today?" she asked.

"Boring," I said.

"Boring? You never said that about class."

"I know, but I didn't participate. I hardly listened at all."

"That's not like you," she said.

"I think I'm getting tired of this semester," I said.

"You'll feel better when you're done with those papers."

"I hope you're right," I said.

I decided to start working on my theory paper, which did interest me, but the work seemed tedious. Pat went into the kitchen and made a pot of coffee. We drank an awful lot of coffee, but it kept us working hard. After a couple of hours, I made us a salad with pieces of ham, cheese, onions, olives, and feta cheese. It was delicious.

"Let's watch a movie," I said. "I'm tired of working."

We cuddled on the couch and watched a French film with subtitles. I thought about Laura and wondered what she was doing. I wanted to make love, but Pat wasn't in the mood. After the film, we went to bed, and again I had trouble falling asleep. I decided that the next day I would call my doctor to get a sleeping pill. In the morning, I felt tired but had to get up to go to class. After class, I went home and called my doctor. He said that I was under a lot of stress, and that I should come in for a blood test. He would prescribe me a sleeping pill. I called Pat and asked her if she wanted me to come over. She said yes, but I took a nap before going over. After my nap, I felt a lot better and was in a good mood. I got to Pat's apartment and found her working away on a paper she had due in a week.

"We're not going to work the rest of the day, are we?" I asked.

"I have to get this done," she said.

"I'm going to listen to music. The doctor says I'm under too much stress," I said.

"That's fine. I'll take a break in an hour."

I listened to Miles Davis and completely relaxed. I closed my eyes, and my thoughts went immediately to Laura. I imagined her naked, giving me a complete body massage. Soon, I fell asleep. I dreamed of making love to Laura and woke up an hour later. I made some coffee, and Pat took a break.

"When are you going in to see the doctor?" Pat said.

"Day after tomorrow."

"If you keep jogging, you'll sleep better," she said.

"I also have to cut down on the coffee," I said.

"Me too."

"You sleep fine," I said.

"I don't have a guilty conscience."

"Neither do I."

"I'm not so sure about that," she said.

"You still don't trust me?" I said.

"No, I don't. Why should I?"

"Why are you always so jealous?" I asked.

"I hear things."

"People always talk. It doesn't mean everything is true," I said.

"They weren't talking before," she said.

"I don't want to get into a fight," I said.

"You're always avoiding arguments. I think we need to have one," she said.

"What good would that do?"

"Maybe it would clear the air."

"I don't think so," I said, picking up my books and walking out the door.

She said something, but I couldn't tell what it was. I didn't care. I knew she was justified in her distrust, and I didn't want to fight. I drove home and thought about calling Laura. I called her as soon as I walked in the door.

"Hello?" she said.

"Hi," I said.

"What's the matter?" she said.

I had another fight with my ex-girlfriend."

"I'm sorry," she said, "but maybe that's good for me."

"It is good for you," I said. "I'm done with her."

"You've said that before."

"I know, but this time I mean it."

"It's better not to make absolute statements," she said.

"I have to make a decision and stick with it," I said.

"I'm not great at making decisions either," she said.

"Do you want to get together for coffee tomorrow?" I asked.

"Sure. What time?"

"How about two?"

"See you then," she said.

"Bye," I said.

I had wanted to ask her to come over for dinner again but figured I should back off a little. She seemed eager to be with me, but I was still skeptical. She hadn't ended it with her boyfriend, and he had been with her a long time.

I turned on some music and made myself a sandwich. I was exhausted from the emotional ups and downs. I ate my sandwich and read while listening to the music. I couldn't concentrate on my reading. I kept thinking about Pat and Laura. I wanted to call Pat and break it off for good, but I didn't have the courage. I decided to work on my theory paper and really got into it for two hours. I called my mother afterwards and said good night. My mother was so supportive. All I had to do was chit-chat with her, and I felt better. I went to bed early and tossed and turned for a long time. I decided to get up and read for a while. I read until I fell asleep in my chair. I woke up in the middle of the night and went back to my bed. I fell right to sleep and didn't wake up until late morning. I was looking forward to having coffee with Laura, and so I took a long shower and shaved.

I made some coffee at home and spent two hours working on my theory paper. I got to the coffee shop early and ordered a decaf, since I was already wound up. Laura arrived half an hour later and was wearing a beautiful dress.

"Don't you look lovely!" I said.

"Thank you. I bought it in Paris," she said.

"Maybe we could take a trip to Italy one day," I said.

"I would love that."

"I have cousins in Rome," I said.

"I need to get away," she said. "I've been working too hard."

"So have I."

"I get depressed when I spend all my time working," she said.

"I get stressed out and have trouble sleeping," I said.

"You can't be cheerful if you're tired," she said.

"I know. I'm going to get a sleeping pill prescribed for me."

"I have trouble sleeping, too," she said. "I think our bodies are very similar in ways."

"We both have mood swings," I said.

"My mood, as you know, is usually down," she said, "but sometimes I'm up for days."

"That's not good either."

"I know. I wish I were normal and were in a fairly good mood most of the time."

"My mother says normal is boring," I said.

"There's no such thing as normal anyway." She laughed.

I looked at her gentle smile as she laughed, and I felt like I could live with her the rest of my life. I thought about Pat for a second and decided I preferred Laura.

"I don't know why I don't get depressed," I said. "I've always had a lot of energy."

"I have energy, too, but I think my childhood has a lot to do with my moods," she said.

"You had a rough childhood?"

"Not that bad, but I felt like my mother never really loved me, and my father died when I was twelve."

"That's tough. I've been lucky. Both my parents always loved me."

She was staring out the window, remembering her difficult days as a child, and I felt true sympathy for her. She looked like she wanted to cry, but she didn't. I wanted to hug her but felt it wasn't appropriate.

"I love you now," I said.

"That feels good," she said.

We were quiet for a long time and simply looked into each other's eyes.

Chapter IX

"I'd like to cook for you again," I said.

"That would be great," Laura said. "Maybe this weekend?"

"We'll make it Saturday night."

"Fine," she said. "Well, I'll see you later."

"Bye," I said.

I felt closer to her than I had ever felt before. I stayed at the coffee shop for another half hour and thought about Laura and Pat. I was almost ready to leave Pat, but I was still unsure about Laura. I thought that if I could sleep with Laura, then I would be able to keep her. I knew that thought was irrational, but I clung to it anyway. I went home and took a nap. When I got up, I felt much better. I studied for the rest of the evening and went to bed early. I thought about Laura while I lay in bed, and I fell asleep an hour later. I had a restless sleep, getting up every few hours, and felt tired in the morning. I showered and had some coffee before going to the doctor's office. The doctor said everything was fine and prescribed a sleeping pill.

I went home and turned on the TV for the hell of it. I watched it until I fell asleep. I slept for about an hour and felt rested when I woke up. Almost out of habit, I decided to call Pat.

"Hello?" she said.

"Hi," I said.

"I'm still mad at you," she said.

"That's all right. You're always mad at me."

"I wonder if it's worth it," she said.

"You love me, and it probably wouldn't be any different with somebody else," I said.

"I'm not so sure. I'm getting very tired of always being angry."

"I'm sorry," I said.

"That's not enough," she said. "You have to change."

"I'm trying."

"No, you're not. That's the problem."

"What do you want me to do?" I said, exasperated.

"I want you to stop dating your professor, for one thing."

"I'm not seeing her. I only ask her questions for my papers."

"Another thing you have to do is stop lying," she said.

"All right. I went on one date with her, but now it's over."

"Sure," she said. "Listen, I'm going to go. Call me tomorrow."

"Okay," I said.

Now I was upset with myself for admitting that I had been on a date with Laura. I knew Pat would have a tough time ever trusting me again. I worked on my paper for the rest of the evening and took my sleeping pill when I went to bed. I fell right to sleep, and I slept all the way through the night. I felt great in the morning. I made some coffee and thought about calling Pat, but I decided to wait. I hadn't felt that good in the morning in a long time, so I sipped my coffee and listened to jazz. After a while, I decided to go for a jog and ran for about twenty minutes. I took a shower afterwards and then went to school.

Laura was wearing tight jeans and a beautiful blouse. She looked hot.

"Hi!" I said.

"Hi." She smiled.

I decided to sit in the back again and didn't say anything the entire class. I waited until everybody left the room and then walked up to Laura to talk to her.

"That was a great class," I said.

"I didn't sleep at all last night. I just winged it," she said.

"I took my first sleeping pill last night, and it worked wonders."

"I should take one, too," she said.

"I've had trouble sleeping all semester. I put myself under a lot of pressure," I said.

"I'm trying to get tenure, so I put a lot of pressure on myself, too," she said.

"Do you want to go home and take a nap?" I asked.

"Yes. Hopefully I'll sleep for two or three hours. I really need it."

"I'll call you later," I said and left.

Every time I talked to her, I felt renewed hope. I drove home after my theory class and thought about Laura. I was getting obsessed with her and thinking less about Pat. I wanted to make love to Laura in the worst way, thinking that I would possess her. When I got home, I took a hot shower and stood under the hot water for a long time. I felt good, but I was uneasy.

I worked on my paper for two or three hours and exhausted my mind. I made myself a salad and ate slowly, thinking about Laura. I watched television for a while and then called Laura.

"Hello?" she said.

"Hi," I said.

"I was hoping you would call," she said.

"Did you get a nap in?" I asked.

"Not really. I'm not used to sleeping in the afternoon, but I closed my eyes for twenty minutes. That made me feel better."

"I recommend a sleeping pill," I said.

"Yeah. I'm going to make an appointment with my doctor."

"How was your afternoon?" I asked.

"I was too tired to enjoy it. I worked until dinner."

"What did you eat?" I said.

"I made a sandwich for myself. I don't like to cook when I'm alone."

"I feel the same way. Saturday, I'll cook you a great dinner."

"Where did you learn how to cook?" she said.

"My mother mostly, but I've also had roommates who could cook."

"I can't cook worth a damn," she said.

"Do you like scallops?" I said.

"Love them."

"I'll teach you how to cook them when you come over."

"That would be great," she said.

"You sauté them in butter, and if you want, add some spices or bacon," I said.

"Sounds delicious."

"I'll talk to you tomorrow," I said. "I have some work to do myself."

"Bye," she said.

She might have been depressed living alone, but she perked up when she talked to me. I decided to write another poem for her. I sat down for about half an hour and wrote a very romantic poem. I had to keep it from being too sentimental, and I finally got it to work. I went to bed early and took my sleeping pill. This time it took me an hour to fall asleep, but I slept through the night. I felt good in the morning but decided not to go running. I made some coffee and called Pat.

"Hello?" she said.

"I'm sorry, honey. I didn't think you would still be sleeping,"

I said.

"That's all right. It's time for me to get up anyway."

"Why don't I call you after your coffee?" I said.

"Good idea," she said.

After I got off the phone, I thought that she had sounded irritated still. I didn't really feel like calling her back, but half an hour later, I did.

"Hello?" she said.

"It's me again," I said.

"What's up?"

"I miss you."

"It's only been a day," she said.

"I took my sleeping pill and slept well, but it's not like sleeping next to you," I said.

"Yeah. I like sleeping with you, too."

"Shall I come over tonight?" I asked.

"Sure," she said. "I have to get ready for school. I'll talk to you later."

"Bye," I said.

I took a shower and thought about Laura and Pat. Laura was like a big sister, guiding me intellectually, and satisfying me emotionally. Pat was more like a younger sister, who was always pestering me. I didn't know how long I could stay with Pat. After my shower, I put on my jeans and a dress shirt. I walked to school and felt the cold air against my face. Winter was coming, and I loved the changing leaves. When I got to school, I walked into Laura's class, determined to participate. I walked to the back of the room and observed without saying a word. I was disappointed with myself. I had never felt that way about a class. Afterwards, I waited until everyone was gone and went up to Laura to talk to her.

"Hi," I said.

"I guess I'm getting used to your not saying anything," she said with a smile.

"I'm sorry, but I really am listening," I said.

"I know. I just wish you would say a few things."

"I will. I promise."

"How's your paper coming?" she said.

"It's finished, but you're not going to like it."

"I'm sure it's fine," she said. "I'd like to talk some more, but I have a committee meeting."

"Okay. I'll talk to you tonight," I said, and left.

I went to my theory class and spaced out the whole time. I was thinking about Laura, and I kept wondering if she was in love with me. After class, I went home and showered again, so I could be ready to see Pat. She wasn't going to be home for a while, so I spent some time working on my theory paper. My personal life kept slipping into my theoretical ideas. I got to Pat's at about four, and she was home.

"Hi!" I said.

"Hi, yourself," she said.

"We're not going to have a fight, are we?" I asked.

"No, not tonight."

"That's a relief," I said.

"I have some work to do. Do you want to work, too, or watch TV?" she said.

"I worked earlier. I'm going to watch a movie."

She went into the kitchen to study, and I turned on the television. Of course, there was nothing on, so I read one of my books. I usually struggled with some of the ideas I was reading. I wanted to discuss them, but I knew that Pat wasn't familiar with them. I wanted to talk to Laura, but I couldn't do that either. I kept reading anyway and took notes.

"I'm going to bed," Pat said at about ten o'clock.

"Me too," I said.

I was looking forward to making love to her, but she didn't want to. That upset me, but I didn't say anything. I took my sleeping pill and fell asleep. I put my arm over her and felt comforted. At least I wasn't lonely. I slept through the night but woke up Pat by rolling over. In the morning, she told me she hadn't slept much because I had awakened her. She was irritated and got right in the shower. I made the coffee and had a bowl of cereal. After her shower, she came into the kitchen.

"What's going on today?" I asked.

"I have class, as usual. What about you?" she said.

"I'm going to the library, then to class."

"Are you going to talk to your professor?" she said.

"No, and will you let that go?"

"I can't help it, Paul. I know you like her."

"I'm allowed to like other women, aren't I?"

"Not that way."

"I have to go. I'll talk to you later," I said.

"Bye," she said.

I hated it when she was irritated. It seemed like we fought all the time. I didn't want to let go of Pat until I had established something with Laura. I went to the library for a while and worked. For my theory paper, I kept thinking about what constituted the present moment. I couldn't come up with anything tangible, except that it was always changing. Sometimes I was in the past, sometimes in the future, and sometimes in the middle of ideas. The present moment seemed to exist, but in different costumes.

I went to Laura's class, determined again to participate. This time, I sat in the front, thinking it would change my behavior. It didn't. Again, I didn't say anything. After class, I said hi to Laura and followed her to her office.

"You didn't call me last night," she said.

"I was busy working on my theory paper. I completely forgot. I'm sorry."

"No need to be sorry, but I like to get your phone calls."

"I'll call you tonight. I promise."

Her office was small but comfortable. Lit by one small lamp, it was intimate.

"What is your theory paper about?" she said.

"Time," I said.

"That's a big topic." She laughed.

"I'd be interested to hear what you think about it," I said, "specifically what constitutes the present."

"Well, I think there's a certain continuity to it. One experience, or moment, leads to another," she said.

"But are we caught between what is becoming the past and what is not yet here?" I said.

"I guess so," she said. "We have to keep moving to stay up with time."

"I'm not sure I understand that," I said, "unless you mean language is in motion and stays up with that."

"Something like that," she said.

"It puzzles me," I said.

"It's hard to pin down," she said.

We talked for another half hour, and then I went home, skipping my theory class. I decided to study the rest of the day, and I didn't call Pat. I couldn't make any progress on my theory paper, and I gave up after a while. I kept thinking about it, though, and got lost in a mire of ideas. I ate a salad for dinner and spent two hours watching a movie. At about nine, I called Laura.

"Hello?" she answered.

"Hi," I said.

"I was hoping it would be you," she said.

"Laura, I enjoyed our conversation earlier. I've been thinking about what you said."

"Did you come up with any conclusions?" she said.

"No. I'm more confused than ever." I laughed.

"It's not hard to become confused when you're dealing with such difficult concepts."

"I know. I'd rather talk about ordinary things."

"What did you do for the rest of the day?" she said.

"I worked on my theory paper, but time is so confusing that I was thinking of changing my topic."

"I read some of that stuff a few years ago, and I got confused, too," she said.

"Philosophy has become so technical. It's not fun any more," I said.

"That's why I concentrate on literature," she said.

"Literature teaches so much about life," I said. "That's why I chose to write a novel, even if it's not very good."

"It's not bad for your first one. You'll get better."

"You're very encouraging," I said.

"Your theory classes will feed well into your literature, I think," she said.

"I hope so," I said. "You're still coming over for dinner this weekend, aren't you?"

"Yes, of course."

"Well, I'm going to go now. I still have a lot of work to do," I said.

"Me too," she said. "Bye."

"Bye," I said.

I felt elated. She was so encouraging. I was already planning on how I would try to seduce her on Saturday night. After our meal, we would sit on the couch, listening to jazz, and I would kiss her. Then, everything else would take its own course. I was so excited that I didn't go to sleep until midnight. I took my pill, but I didn't fall asleep for an hour. I slept through the night and felt pretty rested in the morning. I was going to go running but changed my mind. I made some coffee and sat down at my kitchen table, reading one of my theory books. I had a bowl of cereal and called Pat.

"Hello?" she said.

"Hi," I said.

"I'm really sorry," she said.

"That's all we do, fight and apologize," I said.

"This is just a phase. We'll get through it," she said.

"I don't know. I've never had such a volatile relationship," I said. "We need to trust each other more."

"That is the problem," she said.

I couldn't believe what I was saying. I had turned into such a liar.

"Do you want me to come over later?" I asked.

"Yeah. That would be nice," she said.

"I'll see you tonight," I said.

"Bye," she said.

I took a quick shower and went to school. I got to Laura's class a few minutes early and sat in the back. She came in a few minutes later and simply smiled at me. The class was interesting, but I didn't say anything. After class, I spoke to Laura.

"Hi," I said.

"How did you like the class?" she said.

"I liked it a lot. Sorry I didn't contribute."

"That's all right."

"I like the way you ask questions," I said.

"I hate lecturing," she said.

"Lectures usually put me to sleep," I said.

"Are we still on for Saturday?" she said.

"You bet. I have to go to my theory class. I'll call you later."

"Bye," she said.

It occurred to me that no matter how subtle the differences in our conversations, they were always new. I went to my theory class and spoke quite a bit. I felt confused most of the time and tried to straighten out my thinking. At one point, I realized that confusion was part of the deal. After class, I went home and took a twenty-minute nap. I had a dream that I was making love to Laura and Pat walked in the room. I tried to explain myself to Pat, and Laura took offense. I woke up with a start and went into the bathroom to take a very hot shower. I knew my life was out of control, but there didn't seem to be any way to get it back under control. I decided to call Greg, even though I knew that I wouldn't listen to his advice.

"Hello?" he said.

"Hey, what's up?" I asked.

"I haven't heard from you in a while," he said.

"Well, you can call, too," I said.

"I'm sorry. I've been really busy," he said.

"How's school going?" I asked.

"They're giving me a ton of work, but I'm doing okay," he said. "What about you?"

"I'm not doing that well in my work, and my social life is out of control."

"Sorry to hear that," he said. "I promise I won't give you any advice."

"That's all right. I could probably use some."

"What's going on with your love life?" he said.

"I think I'm getting ready to break up with Pat, but I've been saying that to myself for a while and, hopefully, I'll get serious with Laura."

"At least you know what direction you're going in," he said. "I don't know how you can do it though. It sounds incredibly complicated."

"That's why my work is suffering. I can't concentrate on anything."

"Maybe that situation will get straightened out pretty soon."

"I'm hoping by next semester, I'll be with Laura, and I can do my work," I said.

"What's your mom think about all this?" he said.

"She lets me do whatever I want and doesn't get involved? Why don't we meet for lunch sometime, and I can fill you in on the details?"

"Sounds good. Give me a call," he said.

Greg was a true friend. I knew he didn't approve of my life at that time, but he wasn't too critical. He tried to support me, no matter how bad my decisions might have been. The conversation with Greg motivated me to study, so I read for two or three hours without any distractions. Then I called Pat.

"Hello?" she said.

"It's me," I said.

"Are you coming over?" she said.

"Yeah. I'll be there in a little while."

"Bye," she said.

I took another shower and put on clean clothes. I decided to call Laura because I knew I wouldn't be able to call her later.

"Hello?" she said.

"Hi," I said.

"How are you?" she said.

"Stressed out," I said. "This time of the semester is very difficult for me."

"Me too."

"Well, I can't talk long. I've got to get back to work," I said.

"I understand," she said. "Goodbye."

"Bye," I said.

I got my books together and drove over to Pat's place. I wanted to get laid in the worst way. When I got there, she was cooking dinner.

"Hi, sweetheart," I said.

"I'm cooking chicken," she said, "with asparagus, your favorite."

"You do love me," I said.

"Not really. I like it, too," she said. "How was class?"

"Good. I really got involved in my theory class."

"Great! I know how much you love that class. Food is ready."

"This is real service," I said.

"You don't deserve it."

"How was your day?" I asked.

"Decent. I'm working on a new television show."

"What's it about?"

"It's about economics. It's called *Rising Interest*."

"Catchy," I said.

"I recruited a couple of professors from the economics department, and we interviewed them," she said.

"I would watch that show," I said.

"It's pretty good, if I do say so myself," she said.

"This food is delicious," I said.

"I'm glad you like it."

We ate for a while and talked about various things. She was being sweet and sexy. After dinner, I did the dishes, and she watched television. When I finished, I lay on the couch with my head in her lap.

"Do you want to make love tonight?" I asked her.

"Sure," she said.

She leaned over and kissed me, sticking her tongue in my mouth, and chewing on my lip. I got up from the couch and led her into the bedroom. She put a scarf over the lamp, and I took my clothes off. She started to take her pants off.

"Leave you panties on," I said.

We got into bed, and I already had a hard-on. I started by licking her pussy and inserting a finger to rub her G-spot. I took my time, and eventually she came.

"Oh, that feels so good," she said. "Let me suck you."

She licked my balls and sucked my cock, slowly but forcefully. Soon I came. This time she swallowed it. She massaged me slowly until I got hard again, and then I fucked her. I moved slowly, grabbing her legs and lifting her knees to her head. I kissed her and thrust harder. I couldn't come twice in a row, but I could last a long time. Afterwards, I rolled over, exhausted.

"I like it when you make me come first," she said. "I almost came again."

"Good. You always satisfy me," I said.

We took a shower afterwards and stayed up watching a movie. I snuggled up against her, but I was thinking about Laura. I was so curious about what it would be like to make love to her. Pat and I went to bed early. I was very tired. I had a dream in the middle of the night that took several surprising turns. When I woke up, I wondered how a dream could take a surprising turn if I were creating the dream. It didn't make sense to me. Perhaps there were two levels of consciousness working at the same time. One, a blind unconscious was telling the story, while the conscious was interpreting it. I didn't know what the answer was, but I thought about it for a long time. I told Pat about this dilemma, but she didn't have an answer either.

I was fairly well rested in the morning, and I decided to go for a short run. When I got back, Pat was already showered and ready to go to school. I gave her a kiss goodbye and then made some coffee. I sipped my coffee slowly and thought about Laura. She was so smart. I would ask her about the dream problem. After my coffee, I took a shower and got dressed for school.

I got to school a little early and sat in the back of Laura's class. I looked through my notes and thought about Virginia Woolf. She had always been interested in women, as well as men, and I wondered if somehow that made her more insightful and perceptive. Laura got to class a little late, but she looked well rested. The class was very interesting, but again, I didn't say anything. After class, I spoke to Laura.

"Hi," I said.

"Hi, handsome," she said.

"That was a great class," I said.

"I can't take all the credit," she said.

"You should take most of it."

"Do you want to talk in my office?" she said.

"Sure. I can miss some of my other class."

We walked together to her office, and I felt like I was her boyfriend. When we got into her office, she turned around and gave me a kiss. I kissed her back.

"Do you know what your next novel is going to be about?" she said.

"I have three different ideas. I'm not sure which one I want to do first," I said. "My favorite is about a man who thinks he's a clown. He goes through various experiences as a madman and ends up going to heaven after going to hell."

"That sounds really interesting," she said. "I can't wait to read it."

I thought immediately that she was thinking about me for the long term. We talked for a while longer, and then I decided I had better go to my other class.

"I'll call you tonight," I said.

"Bye," she said.

I went to my theory class and discussed various ideas. I kept thinking about Laura though, and was distracted a lot of the time. After class, I talked to my professor, and he imparted some of his wisdom. I left a little while later and decided to go home. I needed some time to myself, even if I felt lonely. I called my mother and discussed some financial matters. She was very supportive even though money was tight at the time. I was planning to be a teaching assistant the next year, which would pay for school, but for now we were relying on my grandfather's money. I was living in the cheapest apartment I could find, and I never went shopping. After I talked to my mom, I took a nap and slept my usual twenty minutes. Then I called Pat.

"Hi, sweetheart," I said.

"I thought you were coming back here," she said.

"I decided I would be able to concentrate better at home. I have ton of work," I said.

"We always study together," she said.

"Maybe I'll come over later," I said. "I'm going to eat dinner here though."

"Suit yourself," she said. "Bye."

"Bye," I said.

I really wanted to stay home so that I could call Laura. I worked for a long time and was actually able to concentrate. I was thinking about difference and repetition. I knew there were all kinds of repetition, but I realized that pure repetition was impossible. Then, I discovered that pure repetition was impossible because the original and the copy could not coincide in time and space. This was a true revelation to me, and I decided to write my theory paper all over again. After three hours, I decided to call Laura.

"Hello?" she said.

"It's me," I said.

"I knew it was you," she said.

"How did you know?" I laughed.

"Nobody else calls me." She laughed.

"I didn't realize you were so popular," I said.

"I was popular in grade school," she said.

"I wish I had known you then."

"You would have been too young for me," she said.

"We could have had ice cream instead of wine," I said.

"We can still have ice cream."

"I'll get some," I said.

I told her about my new discovery about repetition, and she was impressed. We didn't talk about it for too long though. I didn't want to talk about work.

"What would you like for dinner?" I asked.

"Whatever you want," she said.

"How about pork roast? I can ask my mother how to cook it."

"That sounds great."

"And I'll make instant mashed potatoes," I said.

"You're such a gourmet," she said.

"I'll see you on Saturday," I said.

"Bye," she said.

After I hung up, I imagined making love to Laura after our dinner. I made a sandwich for myself; that was the extent of my meal. I was thinking of calling Pat back, but I decided to wait. I looked over my new theory paper and was very happy with it. After studying, I took a shower and then called Pat.

"Hello?" she said.

"Hi, dear," I said.

"Did you eat already?" she said.

"Yeah. I had a sandwich."

"Well, there's some leftover pasta if you're still hungry," she said.

"Sure. I'll be over in a little while."

I put on my jeans and a dress shirt and drove over to Pat's. It was already dark out, and the moon hung sleepily in the sky. The air was crisp, and I opened my window to feel the breeze. I was feeling better about school, and that gave me a better attitude toward Pat. When I arrived, she greeted me with a smile.

"Hi, dear," I said, giving her a kiss.

"You're in a good mood," she said.

"Yeah. I changed my theory paper, and I'm much happier with it."

"Great! I'm glad to hear it. I hope your stress level goes down."

"I'm starting to relax more already," I said.

"Why don't you have something to eat," she said.

"That would be great," I said.

I sat in the kitchen, and she served me some pasta with bread.

"Thank you, sweetheart," I said.

I ate slowly and looked out the window at the streetlamp. I suddenly felt sad. I wanted to be with Laura. I tried to put Laura out of my mind, but I couldn't. I laughed more with Laura, and now I felt trapped. When I finished eating, I gave Pat a kiss and did the dishes. I looked wistfully out the window and was quiet. It was going to be a long evening, but I was looking forward to the sex. We sat in the living room and turned on the television.

"You're awfully quiet," she said.

"Thinking about my homework," I said.

"Is that all you're thinking about?"

"Yes," I said, irritated.

"Sorry, I didn't mean anything by it."

"Sure," I said. "I'm going home. I can work better there."

"Suit yourself," she said.

I left without saying goodbye or giving her a kiss. My plan was to call Laura as soon as I got home. I drove quickly and had my window wide open. I felt like I was moving closer to Laura, and would be able to break up with Pat soon. When I got home, I composed myself and called Laura.

"Hello?" she said.

"It's me again," I said.

"Hi, you again," she said.

"What are you doing?" I asked.

"Reading."

"I got into a fight with Pat, but it didn't last too long."

"I'm glad it didn't last long."

"I don't think she and I are going to go out much longer," I said.

"I hope not," she said.

"What's happening with you and your boyfriend?" I asked.

"We're taking a break."

"That's good."

"Yeah. I need to sort some things out," she said.

"Maybe you and I will end up together," I said.

"Maybe."

"Well, I'd better get going," I said.

"Bye," she said.

I was glad that she was taking a break from her boyfriend. I was more determined than ever to stop seeing Pat. The night was drawing to a close. I took my sleeping pill, and fell exhausted into bed.

Chapter X

I slept well that night, perhaps because things were going so well with Laura. I woke up feeling refreshed, and I decided to go for a short run after my coffee. After my run, I read for a while, then went to the library. I looked up some books on Virginia Woolf and immersed myself in my research. Two hours later, I looked up from my book and thought I had done enough work. I didn't have class that day, but I knew that Laura was busy until evening. I went home and took a short nap. When I got up, I made half a pot of coffee and sipped it leisurely. I was in love. I decided to call Pat and break it off for good.

"Hello?" she said.

"It's me," I said.

"Don't apologize. I don't want to hear it," she said.

"That's not why I'm calling," I said. "I think we should end this relationship."

"Fine with me," she said and hung up.

My first thought was that she didn't mean it, but then upon reflection, I thought maybe she did. I was determined to let it lie and I tried to put her out of my mind. I picked up a book and read for a long time. Novels often gave me comfort. I made myself a simple salad for dinner and looked forward to calling Laura. As I was eating, the phone rang.

"Hello?" I said, thinking it was Pat.

"Hi!" Laura said. "I thought I'd call you this time."

"That's very nice. I appreciate it."

"How are you?" she said.

"I broke up with Pat, once and for all."

"That's wonderful," she said.

"I'm glad you approve."

"I do. Now I know you're really committed to me," she said.

"I am. I've always been, but the transition is always difficult."

"I know how you feel," she said.

"I really love you, Laura."

"I love you, too, Paul. Well, I'd better go now. I've heard what I wanted to hear."

"Bye," I said.

I was so excited. I could barely contain myself. Now I knew Laura and I would be together. I started thinking about Saturday night's dinner. I wanted it to be perfect. I called my mother and asked her for cooking advice. She laughed when she heard my excited voice. I wrote everything down and decided to go shopping Saturday morning. I stayed up late reading, but I didn't retain anything I had read. I took my sleeping pill, but I didn't fall asleep for two hours. I slept late to make up for the night before, and I got up feeling great. As soon as I woke up, I thought about Laura. I made some coffee and had a bowl of cereal. It was a rainy day, but nothing could dampen my spirits. I was even thinking of going for a run in the rain but changed my mind. I sipped my coffee and watched the business news on TV. I decided to skip my classes, since I would see Laura the next day. I thought about Pat but knew I was done with her. I called Greg to tell him how much my life had improved in such a short time.

"Hello?" he said.

"Hi, buddy. It's me," I said.

"How are you?" he said.

"Much better. I finally broke up with Pat, and Laura is in

love with me."

"That's great," he said. "I guess you're not calling for advice."

"Not really, but I do want to thank you for your support. I can always count on you."

"My pleasure. Is school going better, too?" he said.

"Yeah. I made inroads into my theory paper, which really improved it."

"Great! You'll have to let me read it."

"We'll have to have lunch sometime," I said.

"Anytime."

"All right. I'll call you," I said.

"Bye," he said.

I had always had close male friends who helped me when I was having problems with women. Greg was sincere and understanding. He had had enough difficult experiences of his own. I decided to take a long hot shower and just relax. I was so happy, I sang in the shower. After my shower, I figured I would go grocery shopping for the next day. I spent an hour in the grocery store, buying all kinds of things, and making sure not to forget the ice cream. I went home and took a power nap. When I got up, I worked on my paper for Laura. I still wasn't happy with it. I was feeling pretty lonely; I wasn't used to being without Pat. I was thinking of calling her only to talk but thought better of it. I would have to leave her alone, which would be difficult.

I called my mom out of loneliness.

"Hello?" she said.

"Hi, Mom," I said.

"Did you cook your dinner?" she said.

"No. That's tomorrow night. I broke up with Pat for good."

"I hope it works out for you with Laura," she said.

"I hope so, too. I'll give you more details in a few days."

"See you later," she said.

"Bye," I said.

I went back to work, but I suddenly felt depressed. Even though things were going well with Laura, I had some doubts. I knew how difficult it was to break up with someone, and I feared that Laura would stay with her boyfriend. Now that I had broken up with Pat, I felt vulnerable. I couldn't concentrate on my paper, so I turned on the stereo and listened to jazz. After listening for a while, I decided to write a poem for Laura. I worked on it for an hour until I was satisfied with it. Then I called her.

"Hello?" she said.

"Hi!" I said.

"You're in a good mood," she said.

"I finished a poem for you, and I actually like it," I said.

"You should like it. You're a good writer."

"I'll read it to you," I said.

I read her the poem, and she said she liked it.

"I need to be inspired to write poetry. Novels are so workmanlike," I said.

"I know what you mean. I'll write one for you next week."

"I think I'm going to cut our conversation short. I'm a little tired," I said.

"That's fine. I'll see you tomorrow night," she said.

"Bye," I said.

I wanted to talk to her longer, but thought it would be better if I left it for the next night. I sat in my apartment, listening to music and reading. I read for a while and again realized I hadn't retained a word. All I was thinking about was making love to Laura. I planned the whole thing out then changed my plans. I wanted to start out on the couch, kissing, and then move to the bedroom. I knew things never went as planned, but that didn't stop me. I imagined kissing her neck first, then working my way down. I would give her two orgasms before penetrating her. Then, I would come inside her. I read some more while thinking about sex and fell asleep in my chair. I slept until about two in the morning then woke up and read some more. I had trouble falling asleep the second time, so I took my pill and finally fell asleep. I had strange dreams because of my pill, and woke up in the morning after a nightmare. I got up and tried to decide whether or not I would go for a run. I decided against it. I made some coffee and had toast with it. I was thinking about the dinner that night, trying to make sure I wouldn't mess it up. I wanted to call Pat in the worst way and finally gave in to the impulse.

"Hello?" she said.

"Don't hang up," I said.

"Give me one good reason why I shouldn't," she said.

"Because I have to talk to you."

"What about?"

"I want to stay friends at least," I said. "I know I hurt you, but I still care about you, and I want you in my life."

"You mean you want to fuck me every once in a while, and go out with other people."

"No. I don't think it's fair to you for me to have sex with you, but can't we at least be friends?"

"I don't think so. What would we do?" she said.

"We could go to lunch, or go to a movie sometime."

"I'll think about it," she said.

"Bye," I said.

That hadn't gone well, and I knew I was being an asshole for bothering her. I couldn't help myself. I was worried that things wouldn't work out with Laura. I worked on my literature paper and focused on it for three hours or so. It was starting to come together. I had certainly spent enough time on it. I took a nap for an hour, then started to cook. I put the pork roast in the oven and watched television for a while. Laura was supposed to come over at five. The roast was starting to smell good when five o'clock rolled around. She was late, and I started to worry. She got there half an hour late, but I was so glad to see her. I wasn't mad.

"Hi," I said. "Come on in."

"It smells so good in here," she said, taking off her jacket.

"I don't know what I'm doing, so you'll have to forgive me if it doesn't taste good," I said.

"I'm sure it'll be fine," she said.

"Why don't you sit in the kitchen for a while," I said.

"Okay," she said.

"I've been working on my paper for you, but I know it won't live up to your standards," I said.

"I'll try not to be too tough on you," she said.

"I like my theory paper though," I said.

"That's good. My first book wasn't any good. It takes time to write well about literature."

"I find that writing a novel is easier for me than criticizing somebody else's," I said.

"You'll get used to the criticism aspect after a while. You have to read a lot of it," she said.

I started cooking the broccoli and simply microwaved the potatoes. The roast was almost done, so I took it out for a minute and basted it. A few minutes later, everything was done. We ate in the kitchen, and I was relieved when Laura complimented me on the food. I put on some jazz, which made me feel more relaxed.

"I got in a fight with my boyfriend on the phone," she said.

"What about?"

"You," she said. "He's terribly jealous."

"That's funny. I'm jealous of him."

"Don't be."

"Why shouldn't I be. You still call him your boyfriend."

"Only for lack of any other name. I don't mean anything by it," she said.

"I'm a little insecure, now that I've broken it off with Pat."

"I know how you feel. I think that's why I haven't completely let go of my boyfriend," she said.

I continued eating as if what she had said hadn't bothered me. In fact, my heart had been torn out. I looked at her with a passionless gaze, and hoped she didn't guess how I was feeling.

"Can you handle being with a possessive boyfriend?" I finally said.

"Not really. That's why we were fighting," she said.

I thought I had better change the subject before it seemed like I was being possessive.

"Do you think you'll ever write a novel?" I asked.

"I don't know," she said. "It's tempting, but I'm not sure I have the stamina."

"I'm sure you would finish it," I said.

"I want to write a book of poetry first," she said.

"That would be great. I would like to do that, too."

We finished eating, and I left the dishes in the sink. We went into the living room and sat on the couch holding hands. I told her how beautiful she looked that night and kissed her. After a few minutes, we were stretched out on the couch, kissing.

"You have the softest lips," I said.

"I love kissing you," she said.

"Let's go into the bedroom," I said.

We got up and walked hand-in-hand into the bedroom. I wanted to take my clothes off but decided to wait instead. We stretched out on the bed and our hands were moving all over. She was very wet, and I was very hard. I put my hands down her pants and slowly massaged her clit. She moaned, and I inserted one finger.

"That feels so good," she said.

She put her hand down my pants and rubbed me gently. I stopped her and pulled my pants off. She put her mouth on me and sucked slowly. I came in her mouth; I was so excited.

"I didn't mean to come so quickly. It's going to take a minute to get hard again," I said.

"That's all right. You taste good," she said.

"Thanks. Now I'm going to taste you."

I licked her clit, slowly in circles, inserting one finger and massaging her G-spot at the same time. She came rather quickly, and I rubbed her some more until she came again. By that time, I was hard again, and I mounted her from behind. I fucked her very hard and finally fell over exhausted. I was thrilled.

"That was great," I said, out of breath.

"I agree!" she said. "I didn't think you would be so experienced."

"I think you could teach me a few things," I said. "You're welcome to spend the night."

"No. I'd better go," she said.

"Stay a little while anyway," I said.

"No. Really. I'd better go," she said, getting up from the bed and putting her clothes on.

"I'll talk to you tomorrow," I said.

"Bye," she said, leaning over and giving me a kiss.

I was very disappointed suddenly and wondered if I had

done something wrong. I thought about what I had said and done, and I decided I had done nothing wrong. I tried to go to sleep but couldn't. I took my sleeping pill but still couldn't get to sleep. I wanted to call Pat, but it was too late. I tossed and turned all night and dragged my ass out of bed at eight o'clock. I felt like shit.

I decided not to call anybody that Sunday and simply lay low. I ate a sandwich at noon and went back to bed. I slept for two hours and felt much better afterwards. I watched television. I was too tired to do any work. That night I took two sleeping pills and fell asleep within twenty minutes. I felt so much better the next day. I dreaded going to Laura's class, so I skipped it. I went to my theory class but didn't say anything. I was hurt and bewildered. I went home after class and took a very short nap. I decided to call Pat.

"Hello?" she said.

"It's me," I said.

"I've decided I can't be friends with you," she said, and hung up.

Now I felt really horrible. I read one of my novels and planned how I would handle Laura's class in the future. I thought I might drop the course at the last minute or hand in my paper and not attend any more classes. I thought I would call her first and see what was up.

Chapter XI

I waited until late that afternoon and called Laura.

"Hello?" she said.

"Hi," I said.

"I'm sorry, Paul, for freaking out on you, but I felt very guilty for cheating on my boyfriend."

"Does that mean we're through?"

"I think so. I'm sorry, but I've decided to stay with him."

"Okay," I said and hung up.

I couldn't believe it. My worst fears had been realized. I got depressed for a few days and dropped Laura's class. I was not one to stay depressed for too long, and in the following weeks, I started to feel a lot better. I could actually feel my attitude lifting and my sense of humor returning. I learned how to be comfortable with my temporary solitude and laugh at life's travails.

Lightning Source UK Ltd.
Milton Keynes UK
UKHW011938290622
405159UK00003B/24